"I do not look to you for a wife, ***Fraülein*** **. . .**

It is best that you should know this now—that you do not hope for what is not."

Ruby bolted upright, deep wells of hurt boiling over into fury. "So what have I possibly done to make you think I would want to marry *you*, Wilhelm Morgen? I want to marry a man who can fill my life with flowers and music and light—not pork and Prussian pride and just plain stubbornness!"

She would have stalked off them, terrified that he would see her threatening tears, but Wilhelm moved quickly in front of her, blocking her escape. She froze. Ruby felt as though she were bleeding inside . . . and for some reaason, she was certain that Wilhelm was bleeding, too.

"I am so sorry *Fraülein*," he breathed against her temple. "I am sorry that I made things worse with my clumsy words. It is not *you* I do not want for a wife." His tone beseeched her to understand.

"If this I wanted, you would not be . . . unpleasing . . . to a man. But I am like one already married, even though you cannot see my Oma." Finally he met her eyes. "I carry her . . . here." He laid his free hand on his chest and waited for Ruby to look there, too. "Do you see?"

For Gay

SYCAMORE SETTLEMENT

Suzanne Pierson Ellison

Suzanne Pierson Ellison
March 18, 1986

of the Zondervan Publishing House
Grand Rapids, Michigan

And Ruth said, Entreat me not to leave thee,
or to return from following after thee:
for whither thou goest, I will go;
and where thou lodgest, I will lodge;
thy people shall be my people,
and thy God my God. . . .

[Ruth 1:16]

For where two or three
are gathered together in my name,
there am I in the midst of them.

[Matthew 18:20]

A Note From the Author:
I love to hear from my readers! You may correspond with me by writing:

Suzanne Pierson Ellison
1415 Lake Drive, S.E.
Grand Rapids, MI 49506

SYCAMORE SETTLEMENT

Serenade/Saga is an imprint of Zondervan Publishing House, 1415 Lake Drive, S.E., Grand Rapids, Michigan 49506.

ISBN 0-310-47502-3

Edited by Anne Severance
Designed by Kim Koning

Printed in the United States of America

86 87 88 89 90 91 / 10 9 8 7 6 5 4 3 2 1

In memory of Winston H. Haase
whose life was a parable
for those who would
honor the land,
cherish their loved ones,
and worship the Lord above all.

May his light shine forever.

PROLOGUE

It was the Tree he would miss the most. It stood as tall as ten good men, its crown as wide as twenty. It was the pillar that held up this great stretch of sky, the home that had sheltered his people while the children played and lovers courted and the old people gathered to share timeworn tales in the hot summer air and the cold winter nights. The Tree was timeless; it had a spirit of its own. With quiet dignity it had watched the river buck across the valley and crawl back home again and again and again. With infinite patience it had suckled countless generations of squirrels and wrens and wild mustard weed. Now it would cradle a new kind of people, a people whose time had come as surely as his own had gone.

The solitary man knelt on the massive roots of the Tree and reached out a fraternal hand to grasp the firm rough bark. He would always take comfort in the memory of that one last touch.

CHAPTER 1

It was a sweltering spring afternoon in 1886 when Ruby Barnett saw the Tree for the first time. It greeted her from a great distance as the heaving stagecoach lumbered toward the west, parting waves of mustard weed high enough to hide a horse. Except for the sage-bedded mountains in the distance, Ruby could see nothing for miles but the scraggly, gnarled branches of the Tree, reaching out in welcome like a loving grandma's arthritic hands. For the first time since her father's death, Ruby basked in a moment of genuine peace. Maybe, just maybe, God had a plan for this endless journey after all.

"I ain't never seen nothin' quite like it," the elderly lady on Ruby's right commented, gazing awestruck at the distant Tree. She leaned forward, tugging nervously on the black ribbon that held her sober slate cap in place. "That's gotta be where ya git off, hon."

Ruby nodded eagerly. Uncle Orville had told her it was impossible to miss the Tree and he was certainly right. "About halfway through the valley, the stage will stop by a large sycamore," he'd written. "It's not a real stage stop, but one of our kindly neighbors lives nearby and will be happy to bring you the rest of the way to the ranch." He hadn't mentioned how far the "rest of the way" was, nor what form of transportation Ruby could expect from his widowed neighbor, Wilhelm Morgen. But one thing was certain—anything would be an improvement over the stage!

The train trip from Cincinnati to Los Angeles had been slow, tiring, dirty—and heaven on earth compared to this last leg of the trip. After three days of being tossed back and forth in this primitive traveling cage, every muscle in Ruby's body throbbed. She'd all but given up trying to eat. *I'd rather walk the rest of the way to Uncle Orville's than spend another hour pulled by a team of horses,* she vowed in silence, keeping her complaints to herself. Out loud she asked politely, "Do you see any sort of a town up ahead?"

The widow shook her head, as did the young mother of three who sat on the opposite seat, facing back toward the way they'd come. The unkempt gambler on Ruby's left, who'd laughed when she'd refused to share his bottle, chuckled again at her naïve question.

"There ain't no sorta town ta see, missy. There ain't no town fer another twenty miles, an' we'll be lucky even ta make Caytana 'fore sundown."

Ruby shivered in spite of the oppressive heat. Uncle Orville had warned her—everyone had warned her—that she was going to a part of the country that was not yet fully tamed. But thinking about the west while sitting in the parlor of her snug, lonely house in a modern city of 250,000 souls was a far cry from trundling into the wilderness trapped in a jostling stage! She hadn't had a lot of choices, true. But Ruby had already learned so much on her trip to California that if she had it to do over again, she would have stayed in Ohio and married Harvey Prouty—even though his last-minute offer had come from a sense of neighborly duty, not a heartswell of romantic devotion.

Ruby wasn't a vain woman, but she did have enough pride to believe that someday she'd find a man who loved her with all his heart and soul. At twenty-five, her chances were getting slimmer. But in her quiet way she was certain that if God meant for her to marry, he'd send her the man he had in mind. If he didn't, well . . . she'd still done the right thing to nurse her lonely papa through those last failing years of his life after Mama died.

Abruptly the stage lurched to a stop, throwing Ruby's head back against the stiff rawhide for the last time.

"This here's where ya git off, Miss Barnett," the burly driver above her hollered over the clatter of the creaking wooden wheels. "The resta you folks might as well git out an' stretch a bit. It's a fer piece yet ta Caytana."

Inwardly Ruby cringed; back home no horsecar driver would have been so uncouth as to yell at people sedately tucked inside his carriage. Although what passed for courtesy out here no longer left her open-mouthed, most of the time Ruby still didn't know just was was expected of her. If she refused to talk to men who hadn't been properly introduced to her, everyone thought she was rude and uppity. Worse yet, her position as a woman traveling alone forced her to rely on total strangers, something she would never have done in Cincinnati.

She shuddered as she realized that sometime this afternoon she'd be riding off alone with a man she'd never even met before. Unheard of! Uncle Orville had asked his neighbor to collect her, of course, but Uncle Orville himself was a question mark in Ruby's mind, so that was scant assurance.

Although her memories of her father's youngest brother were warm and friendly, she hadn't seen him since he'd left for the wilds of California twenty years ago. She'd never even met his wife, though her mother had told her once that she'd known Aunt Clara when she was young. Ruby knew from his letters that Uncle Orville was well educated, like her father, which certainly made him a rarity out here. As a woman with a proud high school education, Ruby herself would be even more unusual. Most of her traveling companions on the train as well as the stage had not the slightest inkling of proper grammar, let alone the majesty of music, literature, and art. She wasn't one to look down on these semi-literate folks with sturdy backs and hearts of gold, but being surrounded by people who had no understanding of the artistic visions she cherished only made her feel more alone.

As the other women and the three darling children hurried out of the stagecoach, Ruby straightened her best blue sunbonnet, now dusty from the journey, and smoothed the wrinkled front of her sensible gingham dress. She'd hoped to make herself more presentable before meeting her family—she was a great believer in first impressions—but she knew that it was out of the question. They still used tin washpans for baths in this part of the world, so she had heard, and ironing was a luxury.

As Ruby approached the squat open door of the stage, she could see that the ground beneath her was cleared of mustard weed but little else. Rocks and burrs littered the path to the nearest adobe building; there was no sign of the uneven plank sidewalks she'd seen in Los Angeles. It was getting easier and easier to believe that she'd traveled backwards in time to the first half of the century.

Yet the gentleman who suddenly appeared to help her down from the stage could have been from any century and Ruby would have raised no objections.

His features were smooth and flawless; his laughing eyes a shade of tawny brown. A jaunty black felt hat perched on his head, covering a well-trained shock of matching hair. "Howdy, miss," he told her with a smile that was equally well-trained, appreciative without being fresh as he took in Ruby's rumpled appearance.

In embarrassing contrast, his own fashionable white shirt was the cleanest Ruby had seen since she'd left Cincinnati, and his boots looked as though they hadn't been polished more than an hour.

"Miss Barnett, this here's a friend of yer uncle's," the kindly stagecoach driver told her as he reached up to pull her trunk down from the roof. "He says they're expectin' ya, so I guess yer in good hands."

Thank you, Lord, Ruby whispered to herself. *And to think I almost married Harvey.*

With all the style she could muster, Ruby extended her hand so the gentleman could help her out of the stage. "Thank you so much for meeting me here, Mr. Morgen," she declared with genuine pleasure and relief. "I hope it wasn't too much of an inconvenience."

The handsome man laughed. It was a nice laugh, not judgmental or demeaning, but a laugh that made it clear Ruby had made a mistake.

"I must say, Miss Barnett, this is the first time in the four years Wilhelm has lived in this valley that anyone has gotten the two of us mixed up." He chuckled again, and this time Ruby wasn't at all sure she liked the sound. "Then again, I think Orville's a mite confused himself. I was expecting a little girl of twelve to get off the stage."

His covert appraisal made it clear that he was delighted to find that Ruby was more than twice that age. She was flattered, of course, but she wasn't accustomed to having men stare at her . . . especially men as good-looking as this one.

Ruby knew she was no great beauty, but she wasn't unattractive, either. Her round face had a fresh-scrubbed, wholesome look that was crowned by luxurious ebony hair with a widow's peak. Her tall figure wasn't as lithe as that of many girls, but she had a woman's shapely curves and carried herself with grace and quiet dignity.

The stranger's subtle scrutiny made Ruby increasingly uneasy, as did his knowing, cocky smile and lingering grip on her hand. He was a sophisticated man who had little in common with the boys she'd known back home, and she didn't know quite what to say to him. Suddenly she wished that old Wilhelm Morgen, whoever he was, had been sent to get her, after all. "Don't be put off by his appearance," Uncle Orville had said in his letter. "He's the most decent man I know—all wool and a yard wide." She wondered how her uncle would describe the man who stood before her now.

"My name is Ruby Barnett," she started over, stiffly reclaiming her hand from his encouraging grasp. "I don't believe I caught your name."

He gave her a maddening grin that spoke volumes about his experience with women. "So sorry, Miss Barnett. My name is Joshua Casey, and it is surely a pleasure to make your acquaintance." He took off his hat with exaggerated courtesy. "I own the ranch that borders your uncle's, and our families are the best of friends."

Ruby tried to return his smile as she took hope

again. "Is my uncle's ranch . . . near here?"

He shook his head with a hint of sympathy. "I'm afraid that *nothing* is near here, Miss Barnett," he told her. "That's why we must impose on Wilhelm's hospitality whenever we need to catch the stage." He waved a casual hand in the direction of the primitive structure Ruby had noticed before. "Feel free to wait inside the house until Wilhelm comes. It's almost noon, so I imagine he'll be coming in for dinner soon."

"Wait inside the house?" Ruby echoed, appalled by the idea of ensconcing herself in the home of a perfect stranger who wasn't even present. "I don't think I can do that."

"Sure you can," Joshua urged her, deliberately misunderstanding her meaning as he critically surveyed the building. "It's not nearly as bad as it looks."

Ruby glanced up at him sharply, appalled at the cavalier way he referred to his friend's modest home. But secretly she had to admit that the building itself *was* a bit of a shock. Not much larger than her father's parlor, it looked as though it had been built by some lonely pioneer back when Spaniards and Indians battled for the land. Blocks of hand-tamped straw and clay formed the walls; giant splinters of wood formed some kind of shingles for the roof. The only window was an open square hole that was partially covered with a deerskin. At a distance the tiny house looked just like the barn a few dozen yards to the south, except the barn was larger.

"Pathetic, isn't it?" Joshua continued, his tone more patronizing than kind. "Not bad for a mining camp, but not the sort of place I'd care to call my own."

For some reason his attitude put Ruby out of sorts. This neighbor, this unknown Wilhelm Morgen, was kind enough to deliver strangers to their families in the wilderness and let weary stagecoach travelers stop at his house for rest. And her uncle had spoken of the aging widower with respect; he'd never even mentioned Joshua Casey.

"It looks very neat and sturdy," Ruby heard herself declare. "It would take a man of character to build a house like this all by himself."

"It would take a stubborn German immigrant to build a house like this all by himself!" Joshua countered. "He didn't have to do it alone; we would have helped him." Ruby thought she detected just a hint of envy for the lone settler's courage and independence. "We take care of each other here in the valley, Miss Barnett, but Wilhelm . . . well, he's always quick to help out a neighbor, but he won't take handouts or favors or loans. And he's got no time to jaw with folks; he doesn't know how to play. Wilhelm keeps pretty much to himself."

"Except when the stage comes in."

"Ah, yes, the stage. I myself am on my way to San Francisco on business, which is why I happen to be here this fine afternoon." He flashed her a regretful, inviting smile. "And also why I cannot stay and keep you company until Wilhelm gets back from digging in the dirt." He made it sound as though the old man were grubbing for roots and berries in a breechclout. "Everybody else knows this is cattle country; in all the years that the Jimenez y Rios family owned this valley, they never tried to raise row crops except for the family. Now we've got homesteaders out here trying to raise all kinds of crazy things, pretending their spreads are farms instead of ranches. And Wilhelm—" He shook his head and chuckled. "Wilhelm ate so much hardtack coming to America on that ship that he's determined to grow fresh fruit year round. He wants to bring in some new hybrid orange trees that some fool's trying to grow over near Cayetano. Can you believe that? He talks about running irrigation ditches throughout his whole property some day!" He spoke as though the man were deranged.

"I take it you think his chances for success are limited?" Ruby asked.

He laughed again, a proud, haughty laugh, and Ruby decided she didn't really like him after all. "Wilhelm Morgen doesn't stand a prayer in this valley. He'll never harness that river. It's either bone-dry or flooding, never in between."

He shook his head and looked off across the valley. "Like right now, for instance. We're in the middle of the worst drought in nine years. The land's so dry we don't dare build a branding fire. We pray for rain, but if it comes too fast this fall, the potatoes'll rot in the ground."

Growing more disheartened by the moment, Ruby said, "I'm sure the valley has some redeeming features. My uncle certainly loves it here."

Joshua's expression softened. "So do I, Miss Barnett. Don't get me wrong. If I didn't want to tame this valley I'd just move on. I wouldn't bother to complain. But this land—" his sweeping gesture embraced the endless vista of mustard weed "—gets in a man's blood. I'm a man of letters, and I thought I should live in a town. I tried it for a while, and I can't deny that I enjoy the cultural pleasures that a fine town can offer a man in his leisure time. But there's no city on earth that can compete with the Sycamore Valley at sunset, when the sky paints orange and purple pictures behind this grandpapa Tree."

Ruby found herself staring at the man in disbelief. How quickly she'd misjudged him! Joshua Casey had poetry in his soul. *A man of letters*. She didn't think she'd met a single man since she'd left Los Angeles who actually read for pleasure!

"Time ta move on, Mr. Casey!" the driver hollered as he took the last water bucket away from his team. "I'm gonna try fer Caytana 'fore sundown."

"Miss Barnett, let me move your trunk up to the house. No point in leaving it out here on the ground."

Before she could stop him, Joshua Casey picked up the trunk and started toward the front door. It stuck out awkwardly as he tried to hold it in his arms. He groaned. His face turned red. Ruby was afraid he'd hurt himself.

"Please just leave it outside, Mr. Casey. Mr. Morgen would just have to haul it back out again."

Joshua sighed in relief. "Land sakes, Miss Barnett, I've got a mama and three sisters who dress to the nines and I'm used to carrying their bags. But this trunk feels like its solid pig iron!" He shook his head. "What have you got in there, if you don't mind my asking?"

She did mind. A moment ago she would have minded a great deal more, but ever since he'd verbally brushstroked a sunset for her, she couldn't remember why he made her uneasy. "Books, Mr. Casey," she admitted. "Music books, storybooks, and my grandmother's family Bible." She held out her hands to show the massive size of the Good Book. "I had to leave most of my clothes behind, but I figured they would be the easiest things to replace."

He smiled, and this time it was a nice, natural smile that didn't seem to be rehearsed. "I can't tell you that clothes are easy to come by in the valley, miss, but you're surely right that books are even harder to find—even Bibles. If you're a lover of the Word, you made the right decision."

She knew by the way he said it that he was a lover of the Word himself, and the knowledge gave her comfort. "I don't suppose there's . . . a church out here yet."

He smiled indulgently and pointed toward the Tree. "Revival preachers come through here every six months or so. Spring and fall when the weather's not too bad. Some families have private worship, but—" he shrugged unhappily "we've still got a long way to go."

Despite the sorry picture he painted, somehow Ruby didn't feel quite as abandoned in the wilderness as she had before. A piece of Scripture flashed through her mind: "For where two or three are gathered in my name, there am I in the midst of them." She wasn't sure she liked this man of many faces—especially the way he talked about old Wilhelm—but if Joshua Casey wanted to build a church out here, he'd just found the first member of his congregation.

Joshua opened the door of the adobe house as though he lived there. "Do make yourself to home, Miss Barnett. Wilhelm would want you to feel welcome."

It was a strange choice of words, because nothing in the small hut seemed to welcome her. The kitchen consisted of four wooden boxes, stacked in a pile in the corner, and two straightbacked chairs flanking the roughcut table. Half a dozen iron pots and metal washpans hung from crude nails near the window. A skewered row of whittled men and wild animals lay on the floor near the rock fireplace that jutted out from the wall.

Incongruously, two chipped plates of delicate pink bone china perched on top of the wooden boxes, just as two beautifully hand-embroidered pillow slips, now yellow with use, lay on the squat pine plank bed. They reminded Ruby of the pair of Grandma's pewter candlesticks she'd tucked in the trunk to pretend she wasn't really going to live in the wilderness. She wondered what the austere tenant of this little hut would think if he found them lighting up his table.

"I think I'll stay outside for a while," Ruby decided, suddenly loathe to invade the privacy of the unseen stranger. "I'd like to look at the mountains."

Joshua accepted her explanation with an engaging smile. "It's a view you'll never tire of, Miss Barnett," he promised her. Something in his tone made her wonder if she herself fell into the same category. *I'm imagining this*, she told herself, still unsure whether or not she would welcome his interest. *I'm tired and nervous and I still haven't reached my destination.*

"Mr. Casey! Please!" the driver called out again, the six long reins carefully netted between his fingers.

This time Joshua really did say goodbye. "It's been a pleasure, Miss Barnett. I'm sure we'll be meeting again. And if you remember, would you be so kind as to tell Wilhelm that my horse came up lame and he ought to check it before he takes you out to Orville's place?"

Ruby was shocked. "Why, Mr. Casey, I'd like to help you, but I'm not sure that I should be giving orders to a man I've never even met who's doing me a favor. You said yourself that your ranch is a long way from here, and—"

He shook his head in a way that could have meant he was irritated or amused. "Just tell him, Ruby. He'll know what to do."

He was on the stage and waving goodbye before she realized that he'd called her "Ruby" and she hadn't even rebuked him. In fact, he'd engaged her in conversation so quickly she hadn't remembered that chatting with a stranger was something she'd never do back home!

Belatedly Ruby realized that her traveling companions—almost friends after three days on the stage—were leaving for good and she hadn't even said goodbye. The abruptly severed tie, slim though it was, added to her sense of isolation.

Dust filled the tiny yard as the horses hurried down the rise toward the trickle of water in the riverbed, filling the air with their hoofbeats and whinnies. Ruby watched with apprehension as the stage seemed to shrink before her; by the time it turned back on the main road and passed the Tree, it looked like a child's carving of a wooden sleigh. Even the rhythmic beat of the bouncing stage faded until there was perfect silence in all of the Sycamore Valley.

As the sun-dried stillness overtook her, Ruby tried to focus on the scenery. To the north there was a range of mountains, grayish-green with drying sage and chaparral. To the south a single peak jutted toward the sky, so brown and bleak that not one green leaf or stem seemed to sprout from the omnipresent shedding manzanita. To the east and to the west there was nothing but mustard weed, acres and acres of a surging yellow sea that Ruby was certain no man would ever cross on foot or horseback. Only the Tree rose from the emptiness, like the steeple of a church set out to praise God alone in the wilderness.

She wondered if her Uncle Orville walked close to the Lord as his brother had. She had so many questions about the man and his family! How did they really live out here? How did they cook and clean and sew? How did they worship, and what did they do for fun? And most of all—she swallowed hard with apprehension—did they really want Ruby to come live with them? Or had the offer been a token gesture like Harvey Prouty's, spawned of love for her father and a sense of duty to look after his only daughter now that she was alone?

Alone. Never had the meaning of the word been more obvious to Ruby. Any minute now bandits or bobcats could carry her away in the neck-high mustard weed and no one would ever know . . . or care. She fought back the tears of worry and frustration, but she couldn't deny that she was growing increasingly frightened.

As Ruby lowered herself to sit on the trunk—the only familiar thing in this strange and empty world—all her senses were magnified by an insidious brand of fear welling up inside her. She could smell the sweat of the horses, even though they were already out of sight. She could taste the slightly stale backbite of the sourdough bread that must surely wait inside the adobe hut. She could feel the tiniest hint of an easterly breeze that was salty and cool like the coast.

The undergrowth of the tiny yellow flowers seemed to engulf her; each rustle surely hid a bear, a rattlesnake or a mountain lion. Anxiously she watched the mustard weed, irritated by her fear. "You're twenty-five years old, Ruby Barnett," she chastised herself out loud. "You nursed your papa for seven years and held him in your arms while God took him to heaven and left you behind. Nothing the Sycamore Valley has to offer can scare you any more than that."

A tiny black bird with a hint of red flew overhead while she spoke, and its friendly voice seemed to ease her solitude. Again Ruby studied the Tree, seeking to reclaim the sense of peace it had offered when she'd first set eyes on it. "It's going to be all right, isn't it, Lord?" she asked in the afternoon stillness. "Uncle Orville really wants me, and I'll make a new life for myself here." She repeated the words a couple of times to boost her courage, then she managed to smile.

It was a smile that faded abruptly when the tiny child came screaming past her. He scrambled around the corner of the house so fast that Ruby didn't get much more than a glimpse of him at first, but his shrill voice chilled her. More chilling yet was the sound of the giant man who pursued him, roaring furiously in some indicipherable foreign code.

He looked like a great shaggy bear, with neck-length chestnut hair and a wooly red beard that hadn't been cut in a year. With his heavy build of solid muscle, he could have snapped Ruby's neck in an instant. But he didn't see the young woman sitting on the trunk, so intent was he on running the boy to ground. As atavistic rumblings poured forth from his throat, he charged toward the child with his hands outstretched, shaking the ground with his wrath.

With instinctive maternal courage that Ruby could never explain, she leaped up from her trunk and all but threw herself between the huge man and the little boy. "Don't you touch him!" she hurled at the on-rushing giant, too outraged to think of her own safety. "Don't you touch one hair on his head!"

The man stopped instanteously, dropping both hands to his sides. In a blur of fear Ruby realized that his clothes were handmade and shapeless; he wore a floppy-brimmed felt hat and bulky brown boots made of deerhide. As he stood there staring at her, his thick brown hair fell back into place, erasing the wild neanderthal look she'd imagined. He looked like a farmer, not a madman. In fact, there was nothing the least bit menacing about the powerfully muscled pioneer who stood before her. He looked hot and dusty and bewildered by the sight of Ruby—the mother lioness defending her unseen cub.

Slowly, bravely, Ruby met his eyes. They were sea-blue, warm and gentle—embarrassed and confused. Not a trace of fury lurked in his expression. Although he was Joshua Casey's age—twenty-six or twenty-seven—he studied Ruby with none of the veiled invitation she'd seen in the other man's eyes. She had once read a story about an Indian taming a wild horse with soft words instead of bit and bridle; this farmer seemed to be sizing her up in much the same way. When he reached our in her direction, she wouldn't have been surprised if he'd been holding a lump of sugar in his hand.

"*Komm her, Kleines-Bärchen,*" he ordered, his deep voice fracturing the afternoon silence.

Ruby hadn't the slightest idea what the words meant, but the little boy behind her obviously did. He zipped out of his hiding place and trotted toward the huge man, slipping his small, dirty hand into the other's grasp. Though most boys his age still wore long dresses, he was wearing tiny baggy trousers with red suspenders. Half-ripped hems dangled uncertainly between his knees and ankles. His flour-sack shirt had most likely been white at one time but now was so well dusted with adobe soil that it was a pale shade of gray.

The small boy's eyes were blue like the man's, but more open and trusting as he studied Ruby. His cherubic grin was golden sunshine, a rainbow of welcome for the woman who'd so valiantly rushed to his defense. Incredibly, the exact same smile—twenty years older and muted by the beard—lit up the face of the big man who sheltered the tiny boy at his side.

It was a smile that embraced Ruby so completely

that she could no longer be afraid. She was mesmerized by the blue eyes, the shaggy whiskers, the full lips that curved so naturally to welcome her. It was not fear that knocked her off balance now but some nameless joyous confusion that she had never felt before. She couldn't remember why she'd come to California, and she no longer cared.

The charming grin on the little boy's face was suddenly replaced by a fit of toddler giggles. Only then did it come to Ruby that the boy had never been the slightest bit fearful of the man; the two of them had been playing a game! Ruby could still remember playing chase and hide and go seek with her papa as a child.

Deeply embarrassed by her inexcusable intrusion, Ruby struggled to find a way to explain herself. But she was speechless in the face of the big man's wordless welcome. Something was happening inside of her—something to do with her heart and her lungs. Even though there was nothing left to be afraid of, her blood was streaming through her veins like a snow-capped river during the first spring thaw.

CHAPTER 2

THE MAN WAS THE FIRST to speak, and his deep, booming voice broke the spell he had on Ruby. Even though he did not tip his hat, his tone was straightforward and welcoming. But she had no idea what he was trying to say. She thought she caught the word "Morgen" in the crush of harsh consonants and drawn-out vowels, but then again she was listening for that name. Joshua had mentioned that Wilhelm was German, but surely he'd lived in America long enough to learn at least a little English! But then Wilhelm was a much older man, wasn't he? Or had she just assumed that he'd be Papa's age when Uncle Orville had called him a widower?

It occurred to Ruby that this might be a hired hand from Morgen's homeland; that would account for many things. "My . . . name . . . is . . . Ruby . . . *Barnett*," she told the man slowly, emphasizing her last name in hopes that he might recognize it. "My Uncle Orville told me to ask for Mr. Morgen when I got to the Tree." When he did not reply at once, she burst out in frustration, "Don't you speak any English at all?"

Suddenly his face grew as red as his beard. Ruby wasn't sure if anger or embarrassment erased the playful smile that had heartened her just moments before. "I am Wilhelm Morgen, and you would be the niece of Orville," he declared in slow, labored tones. His "w"s sounded like "v"s; the "r" in his name was a rusty growl. "Your uncle has told me that you would be coming—sometime."

This time it was Ruby's turn to blush as she realized that he'd been speaking English all along! But his accent was so pronounced that she still had to strain to catch the words. "Yes. We weren't—" she slowed down and raised her voice to help him understand "—we were not sure when I would get here. I have money to pay you for taking me to—"

"You do not need to pay me, *Fraülein*," he interrupted, his stilted English jarring her ears. "Your uncle is my friend. And you do not need to speak to me as though I were a man of slow thinking or a very small child. Far better I understand your language than it would appear that I could speak it."

Shame filled Ruby as she looked at the ground. She had berated Joshua Casey for making fun of this stranger for his old-fashioned ways, yet she herself had managed to offend Wilhelm Morgen in less than thirty seconds of conversation! She was alone in the wilderness three thousand miles from home with a rustic foreign farmer whom she'd just insulted. She should have been afraid, but for some inexplicable reason, her greatest regret was that she'd wounded his pride. She already knew that his man would never hurt her.

"I'm so sorry, Mr. Morgen," she tried again, her brown eyes whisking up to meet his blue ones for just a second. "I've been traveling a long time and

I'm not quite myself. I was surprised when you and your son came upon me—" Again she stopped, regretting her candor. She hardly wanted to remind him of the way she'd shouted at him when they first met!

Ruby gave up her halting apology. "I'm sorry," she repeated, holding his steady gaze. "I really am sorry, Mr. Morgen."

To her surprise, Wilhelm managed to smile. It was a gentle smile, a tired smile, not as warm as the first one he'd given her but not as chilly as she probably deserved.

"I know how it is to be traveling for so very much time, *Fraülein*," he told her kindly. "In two days or maybe three, much better you will be feeling."

"Thank you, sir," she answered, surprised at the compassion in those few simple words. "Will you . . . will it be too much trouble for you to take me to my uncle's?"

"I will take you, *Fraülein*," he promised. "But first you would be wanting something now to eat?"

Ruby shook her head, the thought of the stagecoach too fresh in her mind. "No, thank you. But if you and your son are hungry—"

"I do not like to eat when it is hot. Later I will get something for my boy."

As if the mention of the child triggered his memory, he grinned down at the sunny child and squeezed his hand. "This is Kelby. My son," he added softly, as though his entire universe resided in the last two words.

"*Gutentag, Fraülein. Wie geht's Ihnen?*" the boy greeted her politely, his eyes shining with curiosity.

"Speak English to the *Fraülein*," his father corrected him. "She is the aunt of your small friend, Reed. We want to make her feel welcome." His blue eyes, still gentle in a quiet, distant way, carried the depth of his understanding. *I know what it is to be a stranger here*, they seemed to tell her. *I hope it will not be so hard for you.*

Suddenly Ruby wished that Wilhelm had greeted her before she'd met Joshua Casey. Embraced by the warmth of his unpretentious smile, it was hard to feel scared or lonely.

"Where are you from, *Fraülein*?" little Kelby asked in English, his German accent even more pronounced than his father's. "You are from far away?"

Ruby nodded. "I used to live in Ohio. It's a whole summer's ride on a horse. That way," she added pointing to the east. She was going to add that it wasn't quite as far as Germany, but some inner voice prevented her. She sensed that Wilhelm Morgen was eager to leave behind the memory of his homeland.

"I will get the horses," Wilhelm announced before his son could ask more questions. "You may come with me if you like, *Fraülein*, or go back in the house to wait."

"Oh, I wasn't waiting in the house," she assured him. As soon as the words were out of her mouth Ruby wondered if Wilhelm, like Joshua, would misunderstand her. "Mr. Casey said I should, but it just didn't seem right to me."

"Mr. Casey?" Wilhelm repeated, lifting his shaggy brows. "Which Mr. Casey?"

"Is there more than one?"

He laughed, a rich, caressing sound that set her at ease. Joshua Casey had laughed to prove a point, but Wilhelm's natural laughter charmed her like a song. "There are seven in the valley, *Fraülein*, if you count the two who are not yet twenty. But only Joe-David and Joshua come this way to take the stage. The others never come here at all."

He said it as though no one ever stopped by on purpose, yet neither regret nor relief graced his tone. "Wilhelm keeps pretty much to himself," Joshua had told her. Ruby wondered what it was like to live all alone out here. Kelby was a jewel, of course, but Kelby was only a child.

"Joshua Casey was leaving on the stage when I got here," Ruby explained. "He said that his horse is lame and he would like you to look it over at your leisure."

"At my 'leisure?' " he asked incredulously.

"At your convenience," Ruby explained quickly. "Whenever it wouldn't be too much trouble."

He shook his head and offered a shy smile. "I know what this word *leisure* means, *Fraülein* Barnett, but I have never had any. When the Caseys want something from me, they do not often stop to consider what else I may be doing."

Ruby didn't doubt it. Respect for Wilhelm didn't seem to be very high on Joshua Casey's list of concerns. But if Joshua's summons bothered Wilhelm, he concealed it well. "Come with me, *Fraülein*, and we will look at the mare before we go." In answer to her unanswered question he told her, "He always leaves her here with me when he goes away on the stagecoach."

Ruby didn't know whether she should feel relieved or offended when Wilhelm made no effort to take her arm as they crossed the rocky ground. He certainly didn't treat her the way other men did. In fact, he didn't treat her like a woman at all—more like a fawn who'd lost her mother. *Which, come to think of it, is about how I feel at the moment,* Ruby told herself. Compared to Joshua Casey's open admiration, Wilhelm's friendly nonchalance was a relief.

He said little as they strolled past the barn to a large open pasture which was graced by the shade of the Tree. Three horses were dozing near the far side of the fence, two standing and one lying on the ground. Wilhelm whistled, long and low, and the one on the ground struggled to its feet. After a second whistle, just like the first, all three horses started ambling toward the barn.

"It will take them a moment to get here," he told Ruby, speaking as though they were three dawdling children at play. "I have a sick shoat I must check on before we go."

For lack of anything better to do, Ruby followed him into the barn. She wasn't at all sure what customs prevailed in California in regards to traipsing about in a barn with a man she'd just met, but she was certain that Wilhelm had no use for social protocol. His casual attitude soon put her at ease. He talked to the chickens in German and stopped to scratch a cow behind the ears. He spent several minutes with the young pig he'd mentioned. When he picked up the harness for the horses, he tossed it over his chest as though he himself were a beast of burden.

The horses were waiting when they got back to the gate. Deftly, Wilhelm slipped a bridle over the head of a tired looking chestnut and tied her to the fence. He repeated the process on a scraggly black beast who resisted the bit until Wilhelm firmly took hold of her mane and pulled her head down low.

"Kelby, we will need the curb bit for Val today," he told his son.

When the boy stared blankly at his father, Ruby guessed that he must be too young to recognize the difference in horses' bits and bridles. He couldn't have been much more than five or six. But when Wilhelm cast an apologetic glance at Ruby before repeating his instructions in German, Kelby instantly bounded off toward the barn.

"He will learn the English better when there is a school someday where he can go," he explained. "I want for him also to learn the German so we can talk at home."

His eyes said, *So I can talk to someone in my own tongue without apologies and explanations.*

Ruby said nothing as Wilhelm moved toward the third horse, a magnificent gray with delicate lines and a sleek dappled coat. Ruby knew in an instant that the showy mare was Joshua's, yet the horse rubbed against Wilhelm's chest as though he were an old pal.

"He did it again to you, my friend?" he whispered, scratching the mare's nose before he reached for her right foreleg.

He seemed to know exactly what was wrong. With gentle, probing fingers he searched the hoof, digging inside until he unearthed a small pebble. A grimace ripped his face as he tossed the rock toward the barn, but the frown was gone in an instant. Gently he hugged the mare's head as he might cuddle a small child.

Then he asked Ruby, "Did he say how long he would be gone?"

She shook her head. "No, but he did say he was going to San Francisco."

"Good. This time she will be ready before he gets back."

"This time?" Ruby echoed.

For an instant Wilhelm's eyes met hers. "The last time he left her here lame, he was due to return in two days' time. I needed both of my mares for plowing, so I went to the *Rancho* to get another horse for Joshua."

Ruby was touched by his neighborliness, and also by the improvement in his English when he was more relaxed. "How kind you are, Mr. Morgen. You are a very good friend to Mr. Casey."

Wilhelm's eyes flashed with blue fire. "I did not do it for Joshua Casey, *Fraülein*. I did it for the horse." His voice dropped as he added, "He would have ridden her even though she was lame. He has done it before."

It was clear from his tone that riding a lame horse, even somebody else's lame horse, was near the top of Wilhelm Morgen's list of capital offenses. There was a tenderness in the man that belied his massive form and the gruff sound of his Teutonic voice. Ruby marveled that she had ever feared him.

"Here is the curb bit, Papa," little Kelby announced a moment later, holding the steel bar out to his father. "Do you make cookies?" he asked Ruby without a pause.

Wilhelm gave her a look that said "You know how little boys are" before he said, "Your Aunt Clara fills his mouth with good things to eat. She tries to be his mother." Resentment rather than gratitude laced his tone.

"He won't take handouts or favors or loans," Joshua Casey had told her. Did cookies for little boys fall into that category?

"I've never met my aunt," Ruby told him. "Can you tell me what she's like?"

Wilhelm studied her for a minute, his beard shielding a spontaneous grimace. It was obvious that he had a strong and not altogether flattering opinion of Aunt Clara, but he just said simply, "She is not like me."

It could have meant anything, but Ruby didn't dare probe. Orville had written very little about his wife over the years, and Ruby had no idea what to expect. *I should have asked Joshua Casey*, she told herself, remembering his poetic spirit. *He could have drawn a word picture as clear as the sun on that southern hill.*

"I'm hungry, Papa," Kelby said. "Do I get to eat before we go?"

"*Ja*. You take the *Fraülein* back to the house while I hitch up Val and Hedda. Maybe she can help you cut some bread."

"Of course I can," Ruby agreed, holding out a hand for the smiling child. Since Wilhelm was already busy with the horses and had mentally dismissed his guest, Ruby concentrated on the child as she retraced her steps to the tiny house. "What's your favorite thing to eat, Kelby?"

"The pie made of apples!" he exclaimed, then went on to list half a dozen other scrumptious things. Despite his upbringing in isolation, Kelby certainly wasn't shy. Chattering in a curious mixture of German and English, he proudly told Ruby how he helped his Papa work the ranch, scaring birds off the corn and weeding the melon patch. It was obvious that there was nowhere else he'd rather live.

It only took Ruby a minute to cut the boy a piece of heavy sourdough bread and take a dipperful of water for herself. While they waited inside for Wilhelm, she told Kelby about her journey. He was especially fascinated by her stories of the train, since he had never seen one.

"We came here on a boat, *Fraülein*," he declared, using his hands to show it was as big as the Tree. "I do not remember. Papa says I was very small." As an afterthought he tacked on, "Mama started out with Papa on the big boat, but she never got to see our valley. She never got to live on Morgen land." He said "Morgen land" as though it were a country in and of itself. Though Joshua Casey disparaged Wilhelm's horticultural dreams, Ruby was awestruck that the man had carved any kind of farm out of this dry land with a motherless baby underfoot! Surely he'd had some kind of help along the way.

"It was a boat like this, *Fraülein,*" Kelby informed her, hopping over to the fireplace to pick up one of the carvings. "But bigger. Someday I will ride on a boat in the ocean, too."

It was a beautiful carving. The delicacy of the sculptor's touch was surprising; Ruby assumed it had been made in Germany, as surely only the crudest tools were available in California. "Where did you get this, Kelby?" she asked the boy.

"My papa made it for me. All of these—" he pointed to the collection on the floor "—he made for me. When it rains and it is dark outside, he gives me things to play with."

"Wilhelm doesn't know how to play," Joshua Casey had told her. She wondered if Joshua had ever seen Wilhelm pretending to be a bear or whittling small boats to please his darling son.

"I know a story about a great big boat with lots of people. Would you like to hear it, Kelby?"

"*Ja, ja!*" His blue eyes sparkled. "I know all of my papa's stories. You tell me a new one!"

Without asking permission he climbed up on her lap, as though this were the only way a six-year-old could hear a tale. It felt natural to Ruby, who loved small children and longed to have a baby of her own. She put both arms around his chubby waist and started out in a low, engaging tone.

"Well, once upon a time—"

"What does that mean?" he asked, reminding her quickly that his father probably told his stories in German.

"It means that something happened a long time ago. Do you understand?"

He grinned. "I understand, *Fraülein.*"

She laughed. "*Fraülein*" seemed like such a long word from such a little mouth!"

"I don't mind if you call me Ruby."

He gave her a spontaneous hug. "All right, *Fräulein* Ruby. What happened to the big, big boat?"

She held him close and started the tale of Noah's Ark. She didn't know if he'd heard many Bible stories, but this one, so popular with children from Ruby's church in Cincinnati, was apparently new to him.

As his eyes grew huge with the exciting tale, Ruby couldn't help but marvel at how well he'd managed to turn out without a mother. Kelby clearly adored his father, yet he seemed to cry out for a woman's touch. For that matter, so did this tiny house. Even now that she'd been welcomed by the owner, the stark absence of windowglass or flowers or curtains still bothered Ruby. Was it really lack of money that kept the house so bare? Or did Wilhelm Morgen simply have no use for beauty in his life?

Ruby did not know how long he'd been standing in the doorway, but when she came to the last word of the story, Wilhelm's voice boomed through the one-room house.

"We will go now," he declared, in a strange gruff tone that she had not heard him use before.

Ruby turned to gaze up at Wilhelm, anticipating anger or impatience on his craggy face. To her surprise, it was something else altogether that shadowed his roughhewn features—something caused by the unexpected sight of a young woman at his table with his baby boy nestled in her loving arms.

It was grief.

The sun had passed its zenith when Wilhelm Morgen's team pulled his heavy wagon into the oak-shaded lane that led to the Barnett ranch. He didn't like to come here at any time, and he particularly didn't want to come here now. He had agreed to bring the *Fraülein* to Orville because it was the neighborly thing to do, but he would avoid her—and any discussion that linked her name to his—from this day forward.

The Barnetts had more money than Wilhelm—almost everybody in the valley did—but that wasn't why he resisted their friendship. Orville was a good man, a solid man, and he had earned Wilhelm's respect. But the man's meddling wife had taken one look at little Kelby and decided to find the boy a mother whether Wilhelm liked it or not. Anyone would do, even her sixteen-year-old daughter Phoebe, who giggled like a goose at Wilhelm's old-world speech and workman's clothes.

He had expected the niece to be like Phoebe, another buzzing gnat to be swatted away in the rising summer heat. But *Fraülein* Barnett was a woman, not a girl, with fear in her eyes and courage in her heart. What a brave picture she'd made in front of his house, fiercely defending little Kelby from a man nearly twice her size! Few women would have done it. He had to admire her pluck.

The *Fraülein* was almost too old to find a husband, which puzzled Wilhelm. He was no connoisseur of women, but he did not find her unattractive. She had clear skin and white teeth and was built to last through the winter. During the long afternoon's wagon ride she had talked to him when he wanted to talk, but she'd honored his usual preference for silence. To his surprise, she had never complained or used sulky women's charms to beg for favors, which was more than enough to earn his respect.

It also made his problem greater. He could not say to Orville, "This one is too young for me, too silly, too vain, too much in need of a city life I can never give her." Yet how could he tell his friend the truth, without sounding like a man of weakness, still paralyzed by grief? Could he admit how hard it was for him after all this time to watch a young woman in his kitchen, embracing the precious child who had lain in his own mother's arms only once before she died?

The sight had carved Oma's name on his heart with fresh pain, reminding Wilhelm that he was still not ready to take a wife again on any terms, no matter how desperately his son needed a woman's loving touch. Clara Barnett's determination to find him a match only strengthened his resistance. He and Kelby had made it this far alone; they would continue to do so.

As the wagon bounced over the rutted road, his tiny son sprawled across the *Fraülein's* lap, sound asleep in the jostling wooden seat. Her fingertips gently touched his cherub's face as she cuddled him, but her expression remained closed and silent as they rode together.

"We will be there soon," Wilhelm told the woman, embarrassed by the sound of his own voice. Four years he had lived in America, yet his German accent was still so strong that at first she had not even realized he was speaking English! No wonder the other settlers laughed at him. Oma had told him that he would never belong in America. She was right. *Better to be poor with those who love you, Wilhelm, than to live all your dreams alone.*

"You've been very good to me, Mr. Morgen," *Fraülein* Barnett told him softly. "I hope I'll have a chance to repay your kindness some day."

Wilhelm glanced at her in surprise. He didn't even want to see her again, let alone find himself in her debt. She was—well, she was a good woman, a kind woman, and he wished her well. But her presence made him sad. He could not explain why that should be, but he knew that he needed no more sorrow in his life. He did his best to be cheerful for Kelby's sake, wrestling with the boy and playing games like the one she'd caught them at this afternoon. In front of others he would never frolic; if Kelby had had a brother or a sister, or even a mother to warm his life, he would not have allowed himself such levity.

He stole another glance at his sleeping child. Kelby's cheeks were red and damp. Instinctively he reached out to touch his son's forehead, frightened, as always, that some nameless fever would snatch the boy away from him without warning. Wilhelm blamed himself for Oma's death, and he was sure that God had not yet delivered his final punishment. But he was certain that he would sacrifice anything—his land, his dreams, his life itself—to spare his precious son from his mother's fate.

Beside him, the woman flinched at Wilhelm's sudden movement; he met her eyes and found on her round cheeks the same silent tears that must have moistened his son's angelic face.

"What is wrong, *Fraülein*?" he asked artlessly. "Are you ill? In pain? Should I stop the wagon?"

She shook her head as a dull flush lit her features. "It's nothing. I'm sorry."

He studied her for a moment, then looked back at the road. The horses had been here many times before and knew they would soon be feasting in the barn; they picked up speed without whip or whistle. As the wagon hit a large rock, the *Fraülein* was jolted forward. Kelby nearly fell off her lap, but she reached out to protect him quickly without thought for herself. It was Wilhelm who had to seize her by the waist, pulling her back to the safety of the bouncing seat as though she herself were a child. Her large brown eyes grew yet more troubled as they met his with quick gratitude; more tears spilled down her face as she looked away.

It was her pride—not haughty but quiet and dignified—that touched Wilhelm. Ruby Barnett glanced repeatedly at the house that loomed before them, two stories of prime white clapboard that put his own simple hut to shame. But he saw no relief in the young woman's eyes as she studied the fine building, no joy as a little girl a few years older than Kelby came bounding out the front door. It was obvious that the *Fraülein* did not recognize the child.

"Mama! Papa! It's Mr. Morgen!" she called out gaily. "He's got a stranger with him!"

Bravely the *Fraülein* blinked back the tears, trembling, as she heard the word. *Stranger.* And then he knew. For some reason, as private and compelling as his own, Ruby Barnett had traveled halfway around the globe to set down roots in a wilderness with no one to embrace her. She did not know these people who shared her blood; she did not know if they would welcome her into their world, or even what their world entailed. Despite the straight back and uplifted chin, she was afraid. More afraid of this family who would shape her destiny than she'd been of Wilhelm Morgen when she'd thought of him as a charging bear.

Kelby clung to her hand with innocent exuberance, but Wilhelm kept his body stiff as he leaned away. He could not afford to be moved by pity; he had enough grief of his own. He had survived in this hostile frontier. So would she. In fact, she would do better; she would not be alone.

But his own memories smothered him as he saw her apprehension. He remembered Oma's frightened face the day they'd boarded the train in Frankfurt and waved goodbye to everyone they'd ever known. He had held her close and promised her that nothing could hurt her with her brave young husband by her side. Their son would be born in America; their son would sink roots down deep in the new land.

Oma hadn't had the strength for the journey; she'd known it from the start. *The Fraülein is much stronger,* Wilhelm told himself. *She has made it this far without help; a few hours of Clara Barnett's fussing will not do her any harm. When Orville comes home for supper tonight, she will be happy.*

He had done his duty; he'd already sacrificed half a day's work for the woman. He would deliver her to Clara and get back home in time to do his chores.

"They will ask me into the house, *Fraülein*, but I should go quickly," his big voice boomed out across the yard. "It is late and my cow will be full."

The *Fraülein* did not move; she did not answer. Her shoulders stiffened and her breath came in quiet gasps as the door slammed open and shut again and a herd of children streamed out. She squeezed Kelby's hand a little tighter, but she did not even look at Wilhelm. Somehow the tears dried on her face.

He knew how badly she wanted him to stay beside her for just a little while. He also knew she would not ask him.

Wilhelm's chin dropped an inch or two as he lowered his head to speak to her softly. He did not believe his own voice when it made him say, "Unless you do not wish it, *Fraülein*, for a while yet—perhaps I could stay."

CHAPTER 3

RUBY COULD NOT EXPLAIN the relief she felt when Wilhelm decided not to dump her off at Uncle Orville's like a wagonload of hay for the horses. She hardly knew the man, but in some imexplicable way, she trusted him. As far as she'd come, this final moment was somehow the most frightening part of her journey. She didn't want to be left alone.

"Help me, Lord," she whispered, her voice too low for Wilhelm's listening ears. "Let me love these people. Let them learn to love me."

After that there wasn't time for prayer or trepidation. She was overrun with the cluster of children—a matched set of girls, one little boy and a teenager who had to be her cousin Phoebe. A heavyset woman with her pale hair in a bun hustled along after her brood, cackling like a genial hen as she welcomed the new arrivals.

"Wilhelm! How gooda ya ta come. Do come in an' set a spell! An' look at you, little Ruby! Yer the spittin' image a yer ma when she was young! All growed up and all!" She reached up for Kelby, tickling and nuzzling him as though he were a baby. "D ya have a kiss for yer Auntie Clara, hon?" she asked, ignoring his wiggles and squirms. "There's cookies waitin' in th' kitchen jist like always!"

Kelby seemed eager to escape her cloying grasp. With a quick look at his papa for permission, he scrambled off with the other boy—who looked about seven—in the direction of the house. Both girls, sporting long brown braids and long black tights and toothy, smiling faces, gawked at Ruby as Wilhelm helped her down from the wagon. He didn't look embarrassed as he held her chastely; he might as well have been patting a foal. He seemed . . . well, totally indifferent to the fact that he was touching a young woman whom some might have said was moderately appealing. Ruby stiffled her irritation with his nonchalance. *I'm just feeling sensitive right now,* she told herself. *This man has already done more than enough for me.* Besides, didn't she *like* the fact that he hadn't looked her over the way Joshua had?

Wilhelm slung Ruby's heavy trunk over one shoulder as though it were a sack of corn. He said nothing as the gaggle of girls surrounded him, giggling and asking questions as they ushered Ruby toward the house.

"Is this what they're wearin' now in Ahia?" Phoebe queried enviously, glancing from Ruby's nicely fitted bodice to her own shapeless calico. The turkey red suited Phoebe's dark coloring, but the pinafore apron that covered most of the dress was covered with flour and grease stains. Her boots were fashioned from cowhide rather than deer, but they still looked like a crude pioneer effort compared to Ruby's high-top hook and eye shoes. "I can't wait ta hear 'bout ever'thin' in Cincinnata! I ain't never been to a real city . . . not even Las Anglas!"

"I shouldn't wonder," Ruby replied when she managed to get a word in edgewise. "Sycamore Valley is a long way from Los Angeles."

"It's a long way from *anywhere*," Phoebe moaned. "We have to git our mail in Caytana, an' that takes a whole day to go an' come back so we don't go more'n oncet a month. There's jist a gen'ral store an' a stage stop. Not even a reg'lar livery! You'd have ta fall inta th' ocean ta git any further away from th' resta th' world."

"Don't ya pay no 'tention ta Phoebe now," Aunt Clara directed Ruby, tossing one fleshy arm around her niece's shoulders. "We got nice folk here, an' when th' railroad comes through it won't seem sa far ta Las Anglas." She gave Ruby a sympathetic smile. "We're goin' to a barn raisin' next month fer Clayton and Edie Lissen. Then you'll see how much fun Sycamore Valley can be."

"Fun!" Phoebe snorted. "Is goin' to a barn raisin' what ya do fer fun in Cincinnata, Ruby?"

They were on the front porch now, a lovely white expanse covered with some nameless green vine that belied the harsh dry climate.

"Uh . . . we used to have barn raisings in the area," Ruby managed to say, acutely aware of the difference between her own educated speech and the casual sounds of the people around her. "I've never been to one, but I'm sure it will be delightful."

For some reason, she looked at Wilhelm. He hadn't said a word since they'd arrived, except for a nondescript grunt that had passed for a greeting. No one seemed to know he was there except for Ruby, who suddenly longed for the mute understanding of his quiet company.

He didn't smile at her, exactly, but something about the look in his eyes told her that he knew exactly how she was reacting to this barrage of pointless chatter. Her aunt meant well, she was certain, by her garrulous welcome. But it was not Ruby's way, and it wasn't Wilhelm's, either. No wonder he'd said so little about Uncle Orville's family.

They moved into the house—all of them crowding into the entry hall—while Clara and Phoebe continued to compete for Ruby's attention.

"What d'ya think?" Aunt Clara asked proudly, before Ruby had had a chance to look at the house. "Ain't she a beaut?"

The rug was hand twisted from brown and gold rags; real glass filled the windows. A massive wooden table, three times the size of Wilhelm's, filled the kitchen off to the right. Roughcut cupboards and a wood-burning stove were visible through the doorway, with a half-finished quilt top draped over a chair. Calico curtains of red and blue fluttered in the gentle afternoon breeze.

"It's lovely," Ruby said truthfully, wondering why the tiny feminine touches could make such a difference. How little it would take to make Wilhelm's house a home! "It reminds me of my father's house in Cincinnati."

She was speaking of the curtains and the flowers, not the people, but Aunt Clara didn't seem to mind. She gave Ruby another warm hug and mused, "It'll be sa nice ta have another woman ta talk to!"

Her comment brought her a smoldering glare from Phoebe, who had been pouting ever since her mother had sloughed off her negative comments about the valley.

"Is there somewhere Mr. Morgen could put my trunk where it wouldn't be in the way?" Ruby asked, hoping her tactful question wouldn't offend anyone. She couldn't very well fuss over the man, but he'd been standing there for some time with the heavy trunk on his shoulder—not to mention his hat still on his head—and she suspected that he wasn't going to speak to Aunt Clara unless he was forced to.

"Oh, jist leave it by th' stairs, Wilhelm," Aunt Clara suggested, suddenly full of smiles for him again. "Yer such a big, strong, helpful man. I don't know what we'd do without ya here in th' valley." She glanced at her frowning daughter as she said the words, but before Ruby could decipher her meaning, Kelby and the other boy came bounding out of the kitchen, howling as they tried to lasso each other with make-believe lariats.

Ruby watched Wilhelm's face as his son went roaring past, his eyes alight with the joy of having a playmate his own age. A shadow of sorrow . . . some nameless regret . . . darkened Wilhelm's features as he plopped down the trunk. Even then he didn't take off his shapeless hat, which surprised Ruby. Maybe the rules of protocol were different in California, she reminded herself. Or maybe they were different in Germany. More likely, Wilhelm Morgen was a man who didn't pay any attention to games of convention or to the rules that others used to play them. He probably figured that he had more important things to do than listen to women chatter while he doffed his hat.

"I'm Susanna," one of the bouyant girls announced without preamble. Then she pointed to her sister. "She's Kathleen."

The two girls looked like as similar as two peas in a pod, but Susanna was several inches taller, so Ruby doubted that they were twins.

"It's nice to meet you, Susanna," Ruby answered, wondering how it was that somebody in this family had finally decided to introduce themselves. "I'm your cousin, Ruby."

Susanna smiled at the formal exchange, but Kathleen giggled, one hand covering her perky mouth.

"My goodness, child, are we forgettin' ourselves? Ya know I'm yer Aunt Clara, surely, and this here's Phoebe, who's just turned sixteen." She tossed another meaningful glance at Wilhelm. "An' that wild Injun with Kelby is my boy Reed. Hank's fifteen; he's th' one named fer yer pa's other brother, Henry, what got killed in th' war." She glanced at Susanna and Kathleen and ordered, "Go tell yer pa that Ruby's here, girls. An' tell Hank that Mr. Morgen's horses need tendin'."

Again she smiled at Wilhelm, as though she'd just offered him a quarter of land. It wasn't hard for Ruby to see his resistance to the pushy woman. Her heart was in the right place, but she tried too hard. "Phoebe, dear, would ya kindly get some lemonade fer Wilhelm and yer cousin? They've had a hot ride."

Phoebe didn't say a word. She just tossed her head defiantly toward Wilhelm and waited until he declared in his booming Teutonic voice, "Do not trouble yourself, Phoebe." He used her given name as though she were a child. "I am not thirsty, but perhaps *Fraülein* Barnett would care for something cool to drink."

Ruby wasn't sure if that meant he would take his leave now, but she was terribly hot and thirsty and wanted to confirm any suggestion that he made. "I'd love some lemonade, Phoebe, if it's not too much bother," she said with a smile. A moment later she remembered that ice was not a likely part of life in Sycamore Valley. She'd have to settle for anything she could get.

Aunt Clara herded Ruby and Wilhelm into the parlor, reminding Ruby of the first time Harvey Prouty had come calling when her mother was still alive. Mama had hovered in the kitchen, showing up with pies and cakes and comments about the weather every time the silence grew thick. It was a wonder, Ruby decided, that men ever married girls with mothers. It was obvious that Wilhelm and Phoebe hadn't the slightest interest in each other, and Aunt Clara's blatant interference was breeding an unnecessary kind of enmity.

"Why, look at you, child!" Aunt Clara burst out just as Ruby lowered herself into a stiff wooden chair. "Yer face is as red as a bowla churries! Go out in th' kitchen and let Phoebe get ya some cool water before ya git sunstroke!" It was a command, not a suggestion. "I'll find a way ta entertain Mr. Morgen here till ya git back."

With an apologetic glance at Wilhelm, Ruby did as she was told. She wasn't at all sure how Phoebe would greet her out of her mother's hearing, but she was too hot and weary to resist anything that might cool her off.

Phoebe laughed when she saw Ruby in the kitchen doorway. "I knowed she'd do it."

"Do what?"

"Git ya outta th' parlor fer a spell!" Phoebe laughed again, but her lilting adolescent tones did not seek to offend her cousin. "It's ol' *Vilhelm*," she confided in a low tone, crudely imitating Wilhelm's harsh accent. "Ma thinks I oughtta marry him an' she don't want ya te git in th' way! Hah!"

Ruby didn't know what to say. She tried not to let the girl's insensitivity upset her. After all, she wasn't much more than a child. "I take it you . . . haven't set your cap for Mr. Morgen."

Again the girl laughed. "What girl would? He's small potatas an' few in a hill. Besides, he ain't *never* gonna leave here less'n he gives up altogether.

Now Joshua Casey—he's cute as a bug's ear, but Ma says he won't never tie th' knot. But his brother Joe-David is only twenty-two, an' I think it's about time I put a bee in his bonnet." She grinned, pleased with herself. "I gotta git outta here, Ruby, sa I gotta marry up with a man who wants ta better hisself."

Ruby had no response to offer. Having just traveled three thousand miles to reach Sycamore Valley, she didn't really need to hear that living here was unendurable! What she needed was more of Wilhelm's silent strength. If he could survive in Sycamore Valley, anybody could.

"Your mother sent me in to wash my face," Ruby said quietly. "Could you spare me some water?"

Phoebe sobered abruptly, realizing that she'd spoken out of turn. She bit her lip as she plopped the metal pitcher in Ruby's dry hands, then solicitously held out a tin washpan. "I'm really glad yer here, Ruby," she declared with apologetic warmth. "I know there ain't a lotta fellers out here, but I don't fancy none of 'em all that much nohow. Fer myself, that is," she added hastily. 'I'll be glad ta have a friend right here till I can get away."

Ruby knew that in her own awkward fashion, Phoebe was trying to make her feel welcome. She managed to smile at the girl while she washed and dried her face, then quickly returned to liberate Wilhelm.

Aunt Clara had pulled a chair over beside him and was busy bending his ear about some entertaining anecdote of Phoebe's. He was doing his best to listen politely, but Ruby, already attuned to his feelings, could sense his irritation clear across the room.

Before she could break into the one-sided conversation, the front door opened with a bang. The rest of the family—girls, boys, Hank and Uncle Orville—all burst into the room. Ruby didn't have time to get scared again. She wasn't sure what she'd expected her uncle to look like, but she froze in silence when she saw his beloved, familiar features.

He looked just like her father. He had short dark hair, laughing blue eyes and high strong cheekbones that heightened the look of intelligence on his handsome face. The same wave of welcome she'd sensed from the Tree swept over her now, even though the man had not said a word or cast a look in her direction. He was still a stranger whose greeting could deliver her from this purgatory of waiting or complete this growing apprehension that she'd made a terrible mistake.

And then he turned to face her, this daughter of the brother he hadn't seen in twenty years. He was a big man, a strong man, but Ruby watched in shock as his eyes grew moist and red at the sight of her. For a moment he made no motion toward his niece, his body rigid with emotion. For once the female parrots of his family ceased their endless chatter as he studied Ruby's face, shaking his head ever so slowly as one nervous hand tugged on his suspenders. Then, abruptly, he crossed the room and reached out for Ruby as though she were still five years old and he'd gone to California only yesterday.

He didn't say a word; her father would not have spoken either. He simply held her as close as an uncle can hold a grown niece, his eyes brimming with love for Ruby the baby and Ruby the girl and Ruby the young woman who'd come to brighten his life.

Ruby surprised herself by bursting into tears. But this time they were tears of relief, tears of love, tears of gratitude that the Lord had guided her to the right place at the right time for the right reason. This man was family; this man had cherished her father, and he would cherish Ruby. She was not homeless anymore.

"*Ja, Fraülein,*" Wilhelm whispered from somewhere behind her, too softly for anyone else to hear. Then he stood up and took his leave, so quickly and unobtrusively that only Ruby was really aware of the time he'd chosen to go.

Uncle Orville took a moment to thank him and shake his hand. The little girls found Kelby while Hank walked Wilhelm out to the wagon. By the time he turned the team around in the yard, everyone had forgotten all about him except for Ruby.

Her eyes were on Aunt Clara, who was already babbling about when her niece would sleep and worship and help with the family chores. But Ruby glanced out the front window just as Wilhelm clattered by, and to her surprise his face was turned toward the house. He could not have known she was watching him, but for just a second—unless it happened only in her imagination—he deliberately lifted one hand to tip his hat in her direction.

Ruby felt like she'd just won a blue ribbon at the county fair.

The sun was slumping toward the sea when Val and Hedda pulled the wagon up to the barn. Wilhelm milked the cow quickly, then finished his other daily chores with Kelby's enthusiastic assistance.

"Will you carry me, Papa?" Kelby asked when they were finished, his blue eyes flashing mischieviously. He wasn't particularly tired, Wilhelm knew, but he loved playing "horsie" on his father's shoulders.

He loves playing anything at all, Wilhelm whispered with an ache. *He is the loneliest child in the world.*

Wilhelm had been working since sunup without a break, and he'd been having muscle spasms in his back ever since he'd carried *Fraülein* Barnett's incredibly heavy trunk into her uncle's house. But he mentioned neither to the boy as he knelt down in the dust. "Mount up, *Kleines-Bärchen,*" he said with a smile. "No curb bit on your riding horse today. I will go at a goodly trot."

Kelby giggled as he clambered on his father's back, holding on to the chestnut shock of hair. Wilhelm neighed a time or two and tossed his head as a wild stallion might, then gripped the boy's legs around his waist as he led with his right foot in a valiant imitation of a gallop. He was winded by the time he reached the adobe house and more than eager for a dipperful of water. But Kelby was grinning from ear to ear, so the shimmering heat and the lingering back pain meant nothing to Wilhelm.

The sight of a strange rig in his yard, however, triggered brisk alarm inside the big man. He knew every wagon, horse and buggy in the entire valley, and he'd never seen this one before.

"Howdy, friend. You are Wilhelm Morgen, aren't you?" the sleek eastern voice greeted him as he opened the door.

There were two men, actually, but the one who was speaking was squat and balding and had vibrant red stripes on his vest. His coat, custom tailored and flamboyantly new, lay draped across Wilhelm's bed, one sleeve desecrating the pink and yellow roses that Oma had stitched on her hope chest pillowslips with such painstaking care.

"I am Morgen," he answered coldly. "Who are you? What are you doing in my house?"

It was the other man—the tall, slim man in a more sober shade of black—who answered the question. "I am Clint Blackwell, Mr. Morgen, and this is my associate Lowell Jensen." He stood up to reach out for Wilhelm's hand, but Wilhelm made no move to take it. He could not explain his instant loathing for this pair of outsiders. If they'd been poor and hungry, an old man alone or a family of ten, he would have used up a whole winter's supply of venison jerky or a summer's crop of corn to feed them without a moment's hesitation.

This was different.

The hairs on the back of his neck stood upright of their own volition. "I say to you again, what do you want and why are you in my house?"

"Mr. Morgen," the skinny one continued, "We work for the Southern Pacific Railroad, and we're here to make you a very wealthy man."

The uneasiness intensified, but Wilhelm stood his ground. He knew about the power of railroad people. They were ruthless, they were rich, and they had ways of getting what they wanted no matter who paid the price.

"I have no interest in the railroad," he told them bluntly. "I am a farmer."

How many years did I wait before I could say that? he asked himself as he slowly lowered Kelby to the floor. *All my life I wanted to work the soil, to make things grow on my very own land. At last, I am a farmer. I am poor. I am alone, but every day I watch the sun come up on my own land, and I know that I am now a farmer.*

He held the boy's hand as he watched the strangers. Kelby had spent most of his life by his father's side, and he knew, with uncanny instinct in one so young, that this was a time for absolutely stillness. He strove for invisibility beside his father's knee.

The squat man stood up and moved closer to Wilhelm. He slipped both hands in his pockets and pasted an oily grin on his face. "Well, now, son, I can see you're a farmer. I can also see that you're having a hard time of it and you've probably got more land than you can handle. Most of the folks out here do. But we've got a solution to that problem, a solution that's going to make you rich."

Tension roped Wilhelm's chest as he digested the man's simple words; Kelby tightened his grip on his papa's hand.

"Fact is, we've decided to run the rails through these here parts. Time to join Los Angeles to Cayetano and modernize this valley. Folks are looking to homestead land up here, and there's a killing to be made, son. You're lucky you can get in on it right from the start!" His enthusiasm might have warmed a lesser man. "We need a strip of property that runs right through your land, a mile either side of the stage line east to west, and we're prepared to be mighty generous in exchange for your early cooperation."

Wilhelm could not speak at first. He'd come halfway around the world to homestead land that the Southern Pacific Railroad wanted to buy? The valley's road split the very center of his one hundred and sixty acres!

"Now you've got two choices here, son," the shorter man continued. "You can just sell us what we need and hold on to the rest and carry on like you always have . . . or you can sell us *all* your land. With the profit you're going to make, you can start over again somewhere else in grand style."

Wilhelm swallowed hard. A sudden image of Oma filled his eyes; Oma on the ship saying, *Don't you let this stop you, Wilhelm. Go on and live your dream without me. Do it for yourself. Do it for our son.*

"Mr. Blackwell, Mr. Jensen," he stated slowly, determined that his German accent would not get in the way, "I have a third choice which you have not considered. I can tell you courteously that I am not interested in selling to you any part of my property."

The skinny man moved a little closer to the stout one, as though to form a barrier between Wilhelm and the safety of his house. The expressions on both men's faces grew grim and determined. Wilhelm didn't look at Kelby, but he felt the boy move closer, one hand clinging to his father's fingers as the other gripped his knee.

"Mr. Morgen, I'm afraid that holding on to all your property is *not* one of your options. You can agree quickly, and make a lot of money. Or you can give us trouble, and end up with nothing. Either way, we're going to run a railroad line right past that old sycamore." He gestured angrily toward the Tree. His features darkened as he glared at Wilhelm; he seemed to swell to great proportions.

Wilhelm wondered what kind of force the men were prepared to use to back up their words. He wanted no trouble; he only wanted to work his land in peace. He wanted to give his boy something to be proud of. Somewhere to take a bride and raise his own family someday without having to leave his father and go halfway around the world.

He tried again. "I wish no trouble with the railroad," he declared in a voice of quiet steel. "But you do not understand." He glanced down at the tiny boy who stared at him with such faith and hope, ready to pattern his life after his father's next words. "Someday when I am gone, this land will belong to my son, and when he is gone it will belong to his son, and to his son after that. This land that you want for the railroad . . . this land you would take from my son. . . . This—" he repeated with fire in his parched and aching throat, "—this is *Morgen land*."

CHAPTER 4

"YA GOTTA GIT TH' CORNCOBS an' that there clay pota rusty nails by th' extra saddle, Ruby. I got eve-r'thin' else we need."

Ruby could not imagine what broken pieces of dried corncobs and rusty nails had to do with planting a vegetable garden, but she did as she was told. Sixteen-year-old Phoebe was in charge of this operation; Ruby was merely an apprentice.

It was not the first time in the last few weeks that she'd been trained by her cousin to do a domestic task that was as fundamental to California ranch life as breathing was back home. There were so many jobs that involved growing food or creating household items that Ruby had always purchased in a store; even things that she already knew how to do took on a new dimension. In Cincinnati the ladies sewed for pleasure. Quilting was an excuse to get together and talk for hours without the menfolk, and embroidery was an expression of art and skill. Out here quilts were how a family kept from freezing to death in the winter. Nobody had time to add fancy needlework to something as extraneous as a tea towel.

Ruby had put in such long hours since she'd arrived at the ranch that at first she'd felt like Cinderella. But gradually it was becoming clear to her that Aunt Clara was not taking advantage of her position. Unless every able-bodied person on the ranch worked from sunup to sundown, the family would be hard-pressed to survive. Even the children helped: Susanna milked the cow, Kathleen fed the chickens, and little Reed always collected the eggs. Hank disappeared each dawn with Orville and did what California menfolk did on a ranch. They checked the cattle, shoed horses, mended harnesses, fixed pasture gates, went hunting for fresh game—the list went on and on.

"So tell me, Phoebe," Ruby asked patiently, "what do the nails have to do with planting corn?"

Phoebe laughed. She often laughed at Ruby, but then again she often laughed at life. She had an outspoken, mercurial personality. Joyful one minute, floundering in despair the next. She'd hurt Ruby's feelings a dozen times in the last few weeks, but never once on purpose. She always apologized when she realized what she'd done—though often she never realized it at all.

"We're not planting corn t'day, Ruby. This here stuff's fer th' tamatas."

"Tomatoes? Forgive my ignorance, Phoebe, but—"

"The soil here is hard as a rock, Ruby, even in a good year . . . an' this ain't one. The corncobs break up th' 'dobe some an' hold th' water without crushin' th' roots."

Ruby was willing to admit that there might be some logic to that. But as to the rusty nails—

"Them nails does somethin' ta th' tamatas. Makes 'em grow sa big an' juicy ya wanna eat 'em jist like a apple off'n a tree. It's th' rust what does it. Ma could tell ya why."

Ruby decided not to ask her aunt; she just knelt in the dirt and started digging where Phoebe told her to. Some days she just couldn't bear to learn any more about this barren land. There were still nights when she lay in the double bed with her cousin, stifling the sound of her tears. How she missed her father! How she missed so many tiny memories of home!

The only time Ruby was sure she was welcome here was when her uncle was around, which wasn't very often at this time of year. He never worked on Sundays, but after the household Sabbath service which he conducted with such quiet grace, he usually spent the day reading in the parlor or on the front porch as Ruby did. It was the only holdover she could see from his life in Cincinnati. The rest of the family had no interest in literature at all—not even Hank, who was the only one of the children was was the slightest bit like his father.

"Pa said he might let me 'n' you go along ta Caytana next time he goes," Phoebe declared as she buried the corncobs in the ground. "He don't like ta take more 'n' one a us 'cause he needs th' room in th' wagon. Most times it's Hank or Ma. But he knows how much I wanna git outta here, an' he figgers you'll be missin' folks, too."

Ruby was grateful for the thought. She wasn't sure if a trip to homely Cayetano would lessen her homesickness any, but at least it was something to look forward to.

"Tell me 'bout Las Anglas again, Ruby. Ya know I ain't never been there."

"I've hardly been there either, Phoebe," she answered honestly. "And I've already told you that I just walked from the stage to the train. I didn't even spend the night there."

"But ya saw it up close, din't ya? They had nice carriages an' real silk dresses an' them fancy new beaded shoes I heard tell of?"

Ruby nodded. "Well, yes, I guess I did."

"Don't ya 'mind nothin' else?" Phoebe pleaded.

Phoebe was always dreaming of some faraway city, some golden land of bustling crowds with music and laughter and excitement. Ruby had already told her everything she knew about Los Angeles, and also Cincinnati. With a sudden burst of insight she suggested, "I went to Cleveland once. Would you like to hear what I saw there?"

"Oh, Ruby! Would ya tell me? Tell me ever'thin'! What they eat, what they wear! How the menfolk let ya know they're lookin' fer a wife?"

Ruby had to smile. "I can tell you what I saw, Phoebe, but I'm not sure I know anything about the men. I imagine they're pretty much the same everywhere."

"I should hope not," Phoebe grumped. "Considerin' the fellers I know so far I'll like as not end up an old maid."

Ruby shook her head. "I doubt that very much, Phoebe. You're so pretty and so much fun!"

The girl shrugged off her honest compliment. "The Casey boys can git 'purty' 'most anywhere and ol' Wilhelm ain't lookin' fer fun."

"They aren't the only men in the world, either, Phoebe," Ruby answered, uncomfortable with her cousin's grim assessment of Wilhelm. "You're really quite young yet. I predict that someday a handsome young man will ride into this valley who'll make you mighty glad that you waited for him to come."

Phoebe gave her a dreamy smile before she went

back to the gardening. "Don't git me wrong, Ruby. I ain't got nothin' 'gainst th' Casey boys. But th' Caseys never marry young, and besides, I jist knowed 'em all my life. Eleanor Casey—she's just eighteen—she been like my own sister up till last year when she got married ta some rancher up Santa Barbara way. I miss her somethin' fierce!"

A memory scratched at the back of Ruby's mind. "Wilhelm said there were seven Caseys. Or maybe it was seven Casey men."

"Ah, pshaw," Phoebe laughed. "There's more of 'em than I can count. Ellie's got two more sisters older'n her. They both married up with menfolk from San Francisco. Kin to her ma, more or less. There was another boy between Josephine and Eleanor what died a diptheria when he was knee high ta a jack rabbit. Old Harold Casey, Joshua's pa, he took that right hard."

She started to plant a new row and kept on talking. "Now Harold's got two brothers on th' other side a Caytana with a whole peck a kids. We call 'em th' Caytana cousins, on accounta because we don't see 'em much over here 'ceptin' at Joshua's Fourth of July barbecue and Christmas sometimes. His uncles each got a piece a the ol' *Rancho de la Manzanita* what their pa got off'n a Spaniard back in the 'fifties. Real ol' guy . . . he jist passed over a few years back. The *Rancho* had been in *Don* Luis's family for purt near a hundred years."

"And he sold it to Joshua's grandfather?"

"Well, not exactly. They says 'at Harold's pa was a squatter on the south side for a long time, but ol' *Don* Luis didn't pay him no mind. But after th' Land Act come through, th' court said this parta th' valley didn't belong ta *Don* Luis no more. I don't know all the details, but first thing ya knowed, th' Caseys owned th' whole *Rancho*, 'ceptin' fer a piece th' old guy held onta till th' bad dry spell in '77. Wilhelm an' the Jaspersons got it now. Pa bought our ranch from Harold Casey twenty years ago, 'fore he went back ta marry Ma. But he bought it fair an' square with money he earned minin' gold in th' mountains.

Ruby was still pondering that bit of information when Reed trotted by on his buckskin pony, shrieking and waving his hat like a cowboy. She was always amazed to see such a young child riding without a grownup. Then again, much about Reed often surprised her. He was noisy and rough and rarely held still long enough to say more than "howdy" and "what's ta eat." Even though he was Ruby's cousin, she couldn't seem to warm up to him; he lacked Kelby's natural charm. It seemed to Ruby that Reed almost suffered from an excess of mothering, while poor Kelby was starved by the lack of it. She wondered if Kelby had a pony of his own; she couldn't remember seeing one at Wilhelm's place.

She hadn't seen Wilhelm either for almost a month now. There was no particular reason she should have expected to, but for some reason their first meeting—unusual but somehow promising in its way—lingered in her mind.

I've got no call to be thinking about Wilhelm Morgen, she told herself as a vision of his deep blue eyes and shaggy red beard filled her eyes. *I'm just lonesome. I don't know anybody else out here.*

"This—barn-raising we're going to next week," she started awkwardly. "Who—what sort of folks are likely to be there?"

"The Caseys, fer sure," Phoebe answered. "Belinda—that's Joshua'n Joe-David's ma—she always comes to these bees 'n' barn raisin's jist sa she can lord it over all th' resta us." Phoebe giggled. "She's also prob'ly afeared we'll talk about her if'n she ain't there!"

"Why would you do that?" Ruby asked. "I mean, why would you talk about her more than anybody else?"

Phoebe giggled again, amused by some private thought. "Come next Saturday you'll find out, cousin. Once ya meet her, ya won't never ask me that again."

It was still early morning when they reached the Lissen ranch, but half a dozen wagons already filled the yard. The trip itself had been an education for Ruby. In Cincinnati they traveled in horsecars made for a group of people. Here in the middle of nowhere, they filled the back of the wagon with wooden chairs from the kitchen and sat upright, swaying like clothes on a line in a gale force wind. Phoebe had told her that the chairs served a dual function: once they got to the Lissens, they'd need chairs to sit on while they ate and quilted. Ruby had smothered a smile and said nothing.

"That's the Caseys' rig," Phoebe informed her, pointing to a fine new carriage with a matched team of sorrels. "Joshua always drives Belinda an' Joe-David follows on a horse."

Ruby was perplexed. "That buggy looks big enough for three people."

"Oh, it is. It's jist that this here's still wild country, Ruby, an 'ya never know what yer gonna run into. Ya can't chase a bear or an Injun with a carriage, or go fer help in a hurry if somebody's snakebit."

Ruby was sure that her cousin was only teasing, but still she couldn't help asking, "Indians, Phoebe? I know this is California, but this *is* 1886!"

Phoebe laughed. "Ah, I was only rawhidin' ya 'bout 'em being dangerous. But there's still a handful of 'em left. Chumash, they're called, an' they live mostly up on Manzanita Mountain these days. Sometimes they come down an' ask fer work. Most of th' folks don't want 'em around." Phoebe laughed. "Now as fer th' grizzlies, Ruby—"

"Never mind!" Ruby dropped her voice and gave Phoebe a serious look. "Phoebe, I know you enjoy joshing your city cousin at home. But please—have mercy while we're with strangers, will you? I really want to fit in here."

Phoebe stared at Ruby, her green eyes sparkling in the summer morning. She looked surprised and inexplicably pleased. "Ruby, I didn't think you was afeared a nothin'. Mebbe yer jist like us after all."

The two girls shared a smile before Clara started a round of introductions, starting with Edie Lissen, the new bride.

"How are ya'll doin'?" an elderly lady greeted them a moment later, brushing back the single lock of gray hair that had escaped from her plain brown slate cap. "This must be yer new cousin! I'm Sarah Jasperson. Me and my husband live over ta th' northside, not too far from th' Morgen place."

"And not too near, neither," Phoebe clarified. "Takes purt near an hour ta get to Wilhelm's from there in a wagon; half that on a horse. I don't know how he can stand livin' out there all alone."

"Takes all kinds, Phoebe, dear," Mrs. Jasperson corrected gently. "Me and Mo couldn't ask fer a better neighbor." Ruby liked the tone of her voice; she liked her subtle defense of Wilhelm.

"It's a pleasure to meet you, Mrs. Jasperson," Ruby said politely.

"Call me Sarah, gal. Can't stand on cer'mony out here."

A dozen other women quickly clustered around the wagon, each one wanting to get a good look at "the new cousin" and the latest fashions. While they were all gracious and welcoming, their blatant interest made Ruby feel rather like a caterpillar trapped in a glass jar.

Hank helped his womenfolk out of the wagon and carried their chairs into the house. Susanna and Kathleen disappeared immediately, but Reed hung around his mother for a moment or two.

"I don't see Kelby nowhere," he whined.

"For heaven's sake, child! Go play with somebody else till th' Morgens git here!"

"Ya know Wilhelm never misses a chance to help out a neighbor, Reed," Sarah reminded him. "Yer little friend'll be along shortly. In th' meanwhile, ya can play on th' rope swing with Mojer." She pointed toward her oldest boy, who was eleven but didn't mind having Reed follow him around. Phoebe had told Ruby that Sarah had lost her first husband and six children to a band of renegade Apaches in Arizona when she was only thirty. She was getting on in years for a second family, but she was "happy as a clam" with her new life, and no one ever heard her complain.

The women trooped into the house like a gaggle of graylag geese, catching up on every kind of gossip that a community this small could generate. Every woman who was missing was quickly accounted for: one heavy with child, one sick with the flu, one whose stitches were so big they always had to take them out of the quilt after she went home. Ruby wasn't normally attracted to this sort of conversation anyway, but it was harder to look attentive when she didn't know most of the people under discussion.

She could see why Phoebe said that the ladies talked about Joshua's mother. Clad in a store-bought royal blue frock with more lace than was seemly, she enthroned herself in a heavy oak chair while the others brought down the frame from the bedroom ceiling and set it up for the day's bee in the kitchen.

"I believe I'll work on the rose border," Belinda Casey announced imperiously as she studied the Sun and Shadow quilt top, clucking over slight imperfections in the bride's piecework. Nobody challenged her decree.

In a few moments everyone was settled down around the huge square quilt, passing out needles for the younger girls to thread while their mothers spent the day criss-crossing the sunburst–colored squares.

"So you're the little cousin from Ohio," Mrs. Casey proclaimed when Ruby was introduced just before they started to sew. "What do you think of our lovely little valley so far?"

The room grew quiet as every woman in the room waited for an answer. Ruby had the uneasy feeling that her next words would haunt her for years to come. She thought of Joshua's strange greeting at Wilhelm's cabin—a mixture of grand welcome and patronization. She didn't know whether to welcome or shun that kind of interest from his mother.

"I think it's a very special place," she answered truthfully. "From the moment I saw the old sycamore Tree by the stagecoach, I knew this would truly be my home."

Mrs. Casey studied her with narrowed eyes for a moment, then nodded her head in reluctant approval. "My son Joshua is quite taken with that Tree," she admitted. "I've heard him say it ought to be growing on our own land." She flashed a brassy smile all around. "Who knows. Maybe some day it will be!"

Sarah Jasperson and Aunt Clara exchanged a conspiratorial look that left Ruby confused and decidedly uneasy. She was glad when Phoebe handed her a needle, already threaded, and whispered in her ear, "Ya know how ta quilt, don't ya, Ruby? I never thought ta ask."

"So . . . you . . . are happy?" Wilhelm greeted Ruby after dinner, his heavy German accent taking over his English so totally that she cocked her head and strained to follow his words. "I say, do you like it here now," he tried again more slowly before she could embarrass them both by asking him to repeat himself. "Do you like your uncle's ranch?"

"Yes, I like it. But nothing on my uncle's land can compare with your Tree, Mr. Morgen," she answered with a smile, a genuine smile that was almost warm enough to make him smile back despite his vow to keep from becoming too friendly with the *Fraülein*. "I guess everybody here thinks it's very special."

"*Ja*—the Tree, it is special," he had to agree, relaxing his guard just a bit. "But I do not own the Tree, *Fraülein*. This can never be." He paused, wondering how to make himself understood. "That would be like putting a curb bit on the river."

His words felt stilted, awkward to his own ears. With Oma, he had never bothered with English, even though they'd both studied it by kerosene lamp in the evenings for almost a year before they left Frankfurt. For Kelby's sake Wilhelm tried to use the new language sometimes when they were alone. But he and the boy were much happier chatting in German.

Maybe we should go back to Germany, he asked himself for the hundredth time since Kelby had been born. *At least we'd have family there. If anything happened to me here, Kelby would be all alone*. It was his greatest fear. Even if one of these ever-so-distant neighbors should take it upon themselves to care for Kelby if Wilhelm died, how would they know if he were in need of assistance? Sometimes a week or more went by without anyone coming by, not even Mo Jasperson with the bread and cheese his wife made for Kelby in exchange for Wilhelm's pork and barley. If the boy ever tried to go for help as he'd been trained, he could be attacked by a bear or bitten by a rattler—or lost in the mustard weed and never be found.

"You—you have enjoyed sewing with the ladies, *Fraülein*?" he tried again, determined not to sound foolish with this woman he had learned to respect.

Again she nodded, but with less assurance this time. He couldn't help but notice how the delicate pink of her sunbonnet complimented her ivory cheeks. There was such a clean, wholesome feeling about her. She couldn't be less like her scatter-brained cousin Phoebe.

"Yes."

The loneliness echoed in her voice and tugged at some part of his soul. How well he remembered the day he'd arrived in the valley with only a two-year-old barely out of diapers!

"It reminds me of—the times I spent with my good friends back home."

For a moment he was quiet, remembering; then he heard himself admit, "It is hard."

They shared a silent moment of understanding before the *Fraülein* asked him, "Have you seen Kelby and Reed? I promised to tell them a story after we cleaned up."

"Kelby is pretending that fence to climb," he answered, pointing toward a distant corral. "Do not trouble yourself with his amusement."

Instantly he knew she'd misunderstood him. "I promised the boys a story, Mr. Morgen," she replied tightly. "And a promise to a child is an oath signed in blood. I know you're Kelby's father, but unless you have some vigorous objection—"

Before he could answer, Joshua Casey materialized from the motley assortment of tables hauled in by wagon for the day's events. Even though he'd been working on the barn all morning, his assumed position had been more one of supervisor than crewman. His ruffled shirt was still white and unwrinkled. Next to him, Wilhelm felt shabby and soiled after a morning of climbing rafters and pounding square nails. What bothered him most was the uneasy suspicion that if he had not been talking to the *Fraülein*, he would not even have noticed Joshua's fine raiment. He rarely noticed clothing at all.

"Ruby! How delightful to see you again," Joshua greeted the *Fraülein* as though they were the best of friends. "I trust this month of settling in hasn't been too trying?"

Why does he talk like that? Wilhelm asked himself. *Why can't he just say, "Are you happy?" They say there is only one kind of English, but when I listen to him it is just like High and Low German. Does he hope he can talk to the* Fraülein *in a way that I will not understand?*

"I'm getting accustomed to the valley, Mr. Casey," she answered with quiet dignity. "Mr. Morgen was good enough to drive me to my uncle's, and his little son has been very kind to me. I'm looking forward to making other friends."

Wilhelm knew little about the intricacies of English, but he knew that the *Fraülein* had gone out of her way to include him in her conversation with Joshua Casey. Left to his own devices, Joshua would have treated him like one of the Chumash Indians he hired on occasion when no one else would do the work.

"Yes, I'm sure you'll be making lots of other friends," Joshua told her. "I trust you had the pleasure of meeting my mother inside?"

Wilhelm didn't want to hear about the mother. She

was even worse than Joshua. The only Casey he found remotely bearable was Joe-David, who usually bowed to his brother's demands.

"Yes, I met her, Mr. Casey. She spoke highly of you."

Again she does not tell him what he wants to hear, Wilhelm realized. *Does she not understand his position in the valley or is it simply of no importance to this unusual woman?*

"Ah, yes. The feeling is mutual. I take it you've also met my brother?"

"Well, no, I haven't. But—"

"*Fraülein! Fraülein Ruby!*" Kelby was hollering clear across the cavalcade of wagons. "You will tell us a story now, *ja*?"

Wilhelm was ready to reprimand his son for his rude exuberance, but before he could speak the new *Fraülein* gave his little boy a smile that came from so deep in the heart that he knew no part of it was artificial. "I'll be right there, Kelby!" she promised the child. Then she turned back to Wilhelm and told him graciously, "Perhaps we can continue this conversation later, Mr. Morgen." And then, incredibly, she said to the richest man in Sycamore Valley, "You'll have to excuse me, Mr. Casey. Maybe I can meet your brother some other time. Right now I'm afraid I have a prior engagement."

Before Joshua Casey could so much as tip his hat, the *Fraülein* strode across the barnyard to take Kelby's tiny hand.

CHAPTER 5

IT WAS A VIBRANT TUESDAY MORNING about a week later that Joshua Casey showed up at the Barnetts' ranch. Ruby was doing the wash outside in a massive tin tub, counting her blessings that her uncle had put in an artesian well. Many of the other settlers still hauled their water from the river in pails.

"Morning, Ruby," Joshua called out gaily as he slid off his horse. Ruby recognized the mare as the splendid gray that Wilhelm had cared for when it was lame. How angry he'd been at Joshua's cavalier treatment of his livestock! Joshua ground-tied the horse about ten feet from the washtub and sauntered up close to Ruby.

"Good morning, Mr. Casey," she answered more formally, drying her hands on the muslin apron that Clara had given her. "Nice day for a ride."

He smiled ingratiatingly. "You wouldn't be angling for an invitation, would you now, Miss Ruby? Or perhaps hinting that you could rustle up a little something for a picnic?"

"I should say not, Mr. Casey," Ruby answered stiffly. "I was merely making polite conversation."

He chuckled, enjoying her discomfort. Ruby was embarrassed, both by his rather brazen overtures and by the way he made her sound so uppity when she tried to maintain the proper manners she'd been raised with. Back home she knew what to expect from the menfolk—good, bad or indifferent. Here you couldn't tell a thing about a man's worth by the way he talked.

She didn't have much time to dwell on her feelings; quite suddenly the yard was alive with people. Kathleen and Susanna, long braids bouncing, hopped down the steps and greeted Joshua in unison. "Good morning, Mr. Casey!"

"Good morning, girls," he answered, chucking them both under the chin. Lazily he pulled two red peppermint sticks out of his pocket and dangled them in the air. "Looky what I've got here. I don't suppose you know anybody who would take them off my hands?"

The girls giggled as they snatched the candy and galloped off to the barn. Reed, careening down the steps, begged for a treat of his own. Phoebe bustled out onto the porch and batted her eyes at Joshua while she waited for him to speak. Clara, who rarely waited for anything, slipped her generous bulk around her daughter and marched out to meet the new arrival.

"Joshua! How nice ta see ya! How's yer ma?"

"Just fine, Clara. Just fine."

"An' Joe-David?"

"Fit and hearty. All excited over a new rifle my uncle sent him from San Francisco. The latest thing. Would you believe he doesn't even have to reload it to get a second shot?" He turned back to Ruby, the tiniest hint of tension in his suave elocution. "I don't believe you met my brother at the barn-raising, did you, Ruby?"

"How could that be?" Clara burst out, clearly dumbfounded. "We were there all day and introduced ya to ev'rybody. How'd ya miss Joe-David?"

"She had more important things to do," Joshua replied, winking at Phoebe.

Ruby turned back to the wash. *And I've got better things to do now,* her firm stance told him. But Clara would have none of it.

"Good heavens, gal, the wash'll keep. We don't git company ev'ry day. Do come in an' keep Joshua entertained till yer uncle gits in fer dinner."

After the way her aunt had rushed Ruby out to the kitchen when Wilhelm had delivered her to the ranch, she was surprised at Clara's insistence on her presence in the parlor. Maybe she appeared like less of a threat to her marriageable cousin now that she was dressed in Phoebe's cast-off broadcloth skirt and heavy boots. Or maybe Aunt Clara simply valued neighborliness above husband-hunting.

Ruby chose her words with care. She had a point to make to Joshua, but she did not want to offend her aunt. "I'd really like to finish while the water's hot, Aunt Clara. Then I can relax and enjoy Mr. Casey's company without worrying about all the things a body should be tending to on a fine day like today." She flashed Joshua a triumphant smile. Thinking of Wilhelm she added, "Besides, somebody ought to keep that mare company if she's going to be left standing in the hot sun all afternoon."

Across Joshua's handsome face stole a slow flush, subtle but visible to the discerning eye. Suddenly Ruby wasn't at all sure she was proud of her victory. Rudeness was not a trait she wished to cultivate in herself.

"Reed, see ta Mr. Casey's horse now," Clara ordered bouyantly, apparently satisfied with her niece's explanation. "Ya hurry up with that wash, Ruby. Me'n' Phoebe 'll do our best ta entertain Joshua 'til yer done."

"Thank you kindly, ma'am," Joshua replied, holding out an elbow to both Phoebe and Clara so he could saunter in with one of them on each arm. "This is the kind of a home where a man always knows he's welcome."

Ruby joined the group about half an hour later, chastened somewhat by her early encounter with Joshua. While they all huddled in the parlor ostensibly engaged in conversation, she noticed that by and large Joshua did the talking while the women simply listened.

"Hear tell a revival tent is heading this way, Ruby," he informed her. "Nearest thing to a Cincinnati prayer meeting you're likely to find in these parts. I imagine you'd like to attend the service."

"Oh, I'd love to!" Ruby burst out, thrilled at the prospect of an uplifting time of worship. A moment later she realized that she'd fallen into his trap; surely he would take advantage of her eagerness to offer to drive her there himself.

But to her surprise, the cocky expression she would have expected was nowhere on his face. Quite soberly he told her, "I was sure you'd want to hear that good news right away."

Ruby studied his face for a moment, remembering their first conversation about the Tree. She couldn't pin this man down. One minute he talked like a braggart; the next, a man of God. Did he honestly care about her spiritual deprivation out here, her great longing to share with others her love of the Word?

The conversation swiftly moved on to other

things, then ceased altogether when Orville arrived and Ruby joined the other women in the kitchen. She didn't recall anybody inviting Joshua to dinner, but he had no trouble finding his way to the extra chair at the table intended for him. He expressed no surprise when Reed took his right hand and Susanna his left as the family prepared for grace.

"Joshua, would you lead us in prayer today?" Clara asked him.

He bowed in genuine reverence, and his voice completely changed.

"Dear Lord, we thank you for this sterling morning which you have made just for your dear children. We thank you for the wonder of golden poppies on the hillsides and new calves in the meadows. We thank you for the chance to share your love with our cherished old friends and welcome new ones." He paused for a moment, his rich, smooth tones growing even more impassioned. "We are grateful for the good health of our loved ones, Lord, yet I would ask you to gather my mother's heart close to yours this day." Clara squeezed Ruby's hand a little more tightly on the words, and her flesh began to tremble. "Bless this food unto our bodies, Jesus, that we might serve you this fine day. Amen."

Nobody asked about Joshua's mother during dinner. Orville asked if Joshua had heard anything new about the railroad coming through, and Joshua told them about his plans for the yearly Fourth of July barbecue on the *Rancho*. Phoebe chattered on about a dozen inane subjects, batting her eyes at Joshua all the while. He listened attentively, but Ruby couldn't tell if he was trying to make her jealous or merely being polite. He took himself off after dinner, promising to see them all at the revival.

Before Ruby went to bed that night, she prayed for Belinda Casey, although she did not know the reason for her oldest son's concern. She also vowed to make a point of meeting Joe-David at the revival. She regretted her rudeness to Joshua; he really had done nothing to deserve her cool treatment.

It was not until she was almost asleep that it occurred to Ruby that Joshua had told her that the valley revivals were always held at the Tree. With an inexplicable sense of excitement, she realized that Wilhelm would be there.

They gathered at the river—mothers and fathers and grandpas and babies, little girls and little boys and teenagers trying not to preen. A few folks brought their dogs and everybody brought a basket of food for dinner after the morning meeting. Clara packed a ham for the preacher.

He was a portly, middle-aged man with thin, graying hair and a toothy grin that won folks over by the end of the first off-key hymm. His voice was as crusty in speaking as it was raised in song. He gave a sermon full of salvation and repentence, and he seemed to suspect a lot more sin going on in the valley than the ladies had mentioned at the quilting bee.

Still, it was a wonder to gather with so many people—she could have called it a congregation if she'd been so inclined—to worship together in the guise of a church. It saddened Ruby to think that months might pass before she saw the preacher's tent again.

"Is this what you needed?" a mellow voice behind her questioned after the prayer meeting was over. The sound of Joshua's voice, so smooth and strong compared to the preacher's, reminded her of his prayer at her aunt's table. She wondered what kind of a sermon he would have delivered

"I enjoyed it, Mr. Casey. It's not exactly the way we conduct services back home, but—there's more than one way to worship the Lord."

"And more than one way to talk to people, Ruby. Out here it's customary to call a friend of the family by his given name." He grinned beguilingly as he straightened his dust-free felt hat with the same hand that so lazily held his gray mare's reins as he leaned against her. Ruby noticed the tiniest bit of a smudge on his left sleeve and for some reason felt great satisfaction. "No one will think the less of you if you call me 'Joshua'."

Perhaps if she'd heard the slightest bit of humility in his voice, the tiniest hint of entreaty, she might have relented. As it was, his words reminded her of how casually he always treated her, as though they'd been acquainted for years instead of weeks. Not even Harvey Prouty spoke to her so bluntly, and they'd all but shared the same cradle.

"Maybe if you had called me 'Miss Barnett' when we first met, Mr. Casey, I'd feel more inclined to call you 'Joshua' now," she declared straightforwardly.

Before he could answer, the gray mare shifted her balance, causing Joshua to glance down at the animal. Ruby did likewise. To her surprise, one of the mare's front legs was firmly gripped in a big male hand, the hoof tipped back as strong fingers probbed the frog and fetlock.

"She's fine, Morgen," Joshua exclaimed with a touch of asperity as he realized what Wilhelm was doing. "You don't have to keep an eye on all my animals."

Wilhelm shrugged as he put the hoof down. "I do not check the ones your brother rides," he revealed laconically. He glanced up at Ruby as though he had not noticed her there before. "You like to sing," he stated bluntly.

Ruby managed to smile. She didn't like the whipsaw feeling that always gripped her when she stood between these two strong-willed men. Their courteous enmity was impossible to ignore. "Oh, yes, I love to sing," she told Wilhelm. "Back home I was in charge of the choir."

"Were you?" Joshua commented, his eyes taking on a new interest. "Are you—also skilled on the piano or organ, perhaps?"

She shrugged. "I don't know how skilled I am, Mr. Casey, but I do love to make a joyful noise to the Lord with or without a keyboard." A sudden wave of homesickness swept over Ruby. She knew it was an accumulation of many feelings aroused by the revival, but suddenly they centered on the old family pump organ and the new piano she'd played in church. "I used to warm up every Sunday morning with 'All Hail the Power of Jesus' Name,' " she admitted to the men. "I enjoyed the songs very much this morning, but the meeting didn't seem complete without my favorite hymn."

"That's one of my favorites, too," Joshua assured her. She did not doubt the sincerity in his voice. "Maybe we can sing it next time."

Ruby smiled at him, really smiled, before she conceded, "That's a very nice idea, Mr. Casey, but I don't think it would be the same. 'All Hail the Power of Jesus' Name' is a song that can't really be sung a capella." Belatedly she realized that Wilhelm probably couldn't follow all of her words. "It doesn't sound right without a piano," she clarified. "Or at least a little pump organ."

Wilhelm shrugged. "You will never hear this song again if for a piano you wait, *Fraülein*. No one in this valley would haul a five-hundred-pound toy through the chaparral when already the mockingbirds have chosen to live here." He glanced at the lone Tree in the clearing and added thoughtfully, "We have not enough trees for the winters. What we could do with five hundred more pounds of firewood when it grows cold! A piano in Sycamore Valley—a waste of good kindling it would be."

Joshua sent Ruby a look of shared exasperation, and abruptly she was glad he was there. No other person in the valley could have understood the sudden raw ache within her. Whatever had possessed her to think Wilhelm Morgen had special depth? The man was spiritually tone deaf!

"Mr. Casey, is your brother here today?" Ruby she asked Joshua with deliberate warmth. "I don't want to miss another chance to meet him."

Joshua smiled and took her arm. She turned to give Wilhelm a curt goodbye, but he had already disappeared.

"Three times now my stock been hit by that there grizzly," Paul Hanson declared to the circle of men who squatted under the shady shelter of the sycamore. "Carlson's once—O'Rileys half a dozen times since th' last rain. I think it's high time somebody went huntin' fer bear."

Orville nodded, then glanced at Wilhelm. "No sign of him over in your neck of the woods yet, is there, Wilhelm?"

Wilhelm shook his head, grateful for the way Orville always sought to include him in the men's conversations. The *Fraülein's* uncle was one of the very few men in the valley that he addressed by his first name. "It is a long way, even for a grizzly. I do not think he will come."

"No trouble at Jaspersons' either?" Joe-David Casey asked, knowing that Wilhelm was the most likely neighbor to speak for Mo, who was off chatting with the preacher.

"No sign. The coyotes watch the henhouse every night, but that is all."

"Seems like he's staying down in the southeast corner of the valley. Coming down from Manzanita Mountain, I reckon."

Everybody nodded. Of all the men, Joe-David was considered the most knowledgeable about these things. He was a woodsman, a hunter, a cattleman and a horseman *par excellence*. Wilhelm respected these traits, and he respected Joe-David far more than he respected his brother, who had once made the fatal mistake of asking Wilhelm to sell him a section of his land. Still, he did not appreciate the way the *Fraülein* had used Joe-David to punish him for his thoughtless remarks about the piano. He wondered if he would have spoken to her the same way if they'd been alone. Joshua Casey always brought out the worst in him.

"I hear the railroad's already bought up all the land it needs from Santa Barbara to Cayetano," Joshua declared. "Pretty soon we'll be able to get to San Francisco overland faster than by steamer."

Orville chuckled. "Joshua, you've got to stop thinking of San Francisco as the glory spot of the world. I tell you Los Angeles is where the future is. Day'll come when we ship our cattle by rail to that city."

"*Pueblo*," Joshua corrected, using the oldtimer's word that helped San Franciscans look down their noses at the sleepy cowtown. "Just because they're having one of their fits of boosterism down there doesn't mean they'll ever measure up to a real metropolis."

"You've got to excuse my big brother," Joe-David teased. "I'm afraid he's inherited my mother's San Francisco snobbery. Only reason it passed me by is 'cause I was spared going off to college to study journalism."

The men laughed at the joke they'd all heard

countless times before, but Wilhelm thought it was too true to be funny. He suspected that Joshua had always taken after his mother and Joe-David had always been more like his father. He'd never met Harold Casey, who'd passed away shortly before he arrived in the valley, but he'd always heard his name repeated with genuine respect—even by those who weren't awed by a man whose pockets bulged with double eagles.

When the conversation drifted to other things, Wilhelm decided to go find Kelby. He didn't get very far before Joshua Casey called out to him.

"Wilhelm—got a minute?"

Would it make any difference if I did not? he wanted to say. But he had been raised to value courtesy, so he stood his ground. "How can I be of help to you, Mr. Casey?" he asked politely.

Joshua shook his head, then thrust both hands in his pockets. His gold watch chain seemed to bulge with ostentation. "Wilhelm, I don't rightly know how to say this, but . . . I think you should be warned."

"Warned?"

The other man sighed; he almost looked uncertain. "Look, Morgen, I know you don't trust me any farther than you can throw a bull by its tail, but I think you should know that there was a real old fellow on the other side of Cayetano who was just as stubborn about selling to the railroad as I figure you're going to be. His oldest boy told one of my cousins that he'd be willing to sell once his pa passed on."

Wilhelm waited.

"Well, two weeks later, they found the old man dead about a mile out of town. Big gash on the head . . . no sign of his horse. He could have been thrown, but . . . he could have been hit on the head."

Wilhelm looked straight at Joshua, unflinching. "I am sorry he is dead."

Joshua shifted uncomfortably. "These people are serious, Wilhelm."

"So am I, Mr. Casey! For this—" his sudden angry gesture included the assembly of joyful worshippers "—I will always share my land. For Christ's church I would proudly give it away! But not one acre will I sell to the railroad, Mr. Casey. Not today, not tomorrow . . . no matter how much you want to see a city grow beneath this mighty Tree! No matter how old I may grow someday to be, not one piece of track will ever cross Morgen land."

He found Kelby near the river, which was no great surprise; the boy often filled his lonely days there throwing rocks and collecting frogs and talking to make-believe friends. Usually he took advantage of these rare gatherings to play with Reed Barnett and Mojer Jasperson and any other boy who came his way. But this afternoon, for no accountable reason, he was cuddled up next to Orville's niece, side by side against the Tree.

This time she wasn't telling him a story. They were discussing the size of the Tree, how large it might grow, how long it had been there—all things that Wilhelm had told the boy a dozen times, so why did he need to hear it from a woman? He pushed away the obvious answer and forced himself to intrude.

"Forgive me, *Fraülein*," he told her stiffly, "but it is time for my son to come home."

She stood up quickly, awkwardly, brushing the leaves from her quiet blue shirtwaist. Its simplicity suited her, and Wilhelm found himself wondering once more why it was that she was not married. Obviously Joshua Casey was interested in her, and he was a man who showed interest only if it pleased him. Kelby, on the other hand, had known so few women that he ususally didn't know quite what to make of them, but he had taken to the *Fraülein* like a bear to a tree full of honey. As he watched the look of dejection pass his small son's face, he regretted his untimely interruption. He also regretted his callous remarks to the woman a few minutes earlier.

"*Fraülein*," he heard himself saying, his eyes avoiding hers, "I did not mean to be so . . . without feeling for . . . what you may be feeling here." He cursed his clumsy sentence and longed to express himself in his native tongue. He understood almost everything he read or heard in English, but he'd spent very little time unfurling his deepest thoughts in this alien language. She was watching him now, uncertain of his intended meaning. She wasn't even sure if he was done speaking.

"What I mean to say, *Fraülein* Barnett," he stumbled yet again, "is that I do not . . . how do you say . . . have the ear to know this kind of music or that kind. Like a cow whose bag is too full do I sing. To me there is music that people make and music that I hear from creatures with feathered wings, and it is this kind I like better." He sighed, watching her troubled face, knowing it was not enough. He probably had made things worse.

"But for you, I do see that it is not this way, so I am sorry."

Her expression warmed, ever so slightly, as he finally blurted out, "Each time, when the meeting is over, when we sing and pray and read the Word in this strange-for-me tongue, I go back to my house alone and say the Prayer of our Lord in German. Only then do I feel that I have spent that precious hour with my God."

He had never revealed that private spiritual need to anyone before, not even Kelby, and he had no idea why he had done so now. He waited for the *Fraülein* to laugh or look embarrassed; but her reaction was something he had not expected.

"I do understand, Mr. Morgen," she whispered huskily, gripping his arm with her gentle hand. "Truly I do." And then, to his amazement, her eyes filled with tears.

CHAPTER 6

"OH, ELLIE! I MISSED YA SA MUCH!"

There was no denying the joy in Phoebe's voice as she greeted her childhood friend. Ever since Joe-David had dropped by on his way back from hunting bighorn on Manzanita Mountain with the news that his sister had arrived for a visit, Phoebe had been in a dither. Joshua had sent word by way of his brother that he would come by for Phoebe and her cousin the next morning to take them to the *Rancho*.

It was Joshua who made the introductions. "Eleanor, this is Phoebe's cousin from Cincinnati. I think you two will find that you have a lot in common." There was a tone in his voice which irritated Ruby, though she couldn't really put her finger on the reason why. He'd been gracious in his hospitality, warm but not as flagrantly brazen as he'd been before the revival. Still, it troubled her that he'd arranged this visit without ever asking Ruby if she wanted to come; he'd just assumed that she'd be delighted to visit his home. And now, as he introduced her to his lovely and fashionable sister, it was clear that he *assumed* the two would like each other—largely because he wanted it that way.

"It's too bad you can't stay on until the barbecue, Ellie," he said to his sister. "You'll miss C.W. Warren. He's going to stop by here for a few weeks on his way to Los Angeles." He took a moment to tell his guests, "C.W. is a friend of mine from college—distant kin of my mother's in San Francisco," before he returned his attention to Ellie. "His uncle's going to retire soon, so C.W. will be taking over the bank."

"Maybe we can work something out, Joshua. It would be nice to see C.W. again," Eleanor told him, then flashed a smile at Phoebe. "Almost as nice as seeing Phoebe!"

Joshua gave both Eleanor and Phoebe a quick hug, as though both were his little sisters. It occurred to Ruby that he probably chuckled inside whenever Phoebe practiced her artless flirtation with him, but he was always kind enough to pretend to take her seriously. "These two will have a lot to catch up on, Ruby. Why don't we let them chat for a while while I show you around?"

"What a charming notion, Joshua," his pristine mother seconded his suggestion. "We wouldn't want dear Ruby bored with conversation about all the people here she doesn't know and has never heard of."

Her cloying smile didn't do much for Ruby's self-assurance; it was obvious she was being dismissed. She couldn't stifle her sense of disappointment. Even though she didn't care much for Mrs. Casey's high-handed ways, she'd looked forward to some conversation with a woman who had *some* idea of the social standards she was accustomed to—someone who'd read a newspaper within the last year! She'd especially looked forward to meeting Eleanor, who'd given Ruby a swift, meaningless smile before she'd turned her attention back to Phoebe. Despite Phoebe's obvious cultural limitations in this family of wealth and generous education, she was welcomed here in a way that Ruby, the outsider, would never be.

"Let me show you the rest of the house, Ruby," Joshua declared as he offered her his elbow. "It was built by the first Jimenez y Rios back in 1798. Of course we've remodeled considerably since then, but in its day it was the finest hacienda for a hundred miles in each direction."

And probably still is, his tone implied. After seeing Wilhelm's hut, Ruby had been amazed that Joshua also lived in a house made of adobe; but it was obvious that this building had been crafted with a vision toward infinite generations of *Californios*. She couldn't help but think it sad that their time had come to an end.

Joshua showed her more of the house than she would have expected, especially the sparkling clean kitchen which was three times the size of Aunt Clara's and came equipped with a diligent but sad-eyed Mexican servant. "When the Jimenez y Rios family lived here, all the cooking was done outside over a massive adobe pit. We still use it for special holidays like the Fourth of July." His tone grew saucy. "We always have games for the children—potato sack races and the like—and the finest dinner Conchita can provide. My father made it a habit to have at least one surprise in the entertainment, and I've kept to that tradition. Wild horses couldn't drag this year's secret out of me. I haven't even told Joe-David."

Ruby didn't want to show too much interest in his surprise, largely because she thought he was doing a good enough job tooting his own horn without having her join the band. Still, she had to admit that she was looking forward to the barbecue. She was starting to share Phoebe's lament of how little there was to do in Sycamore Valley.

Joshua showed her the cow barn, the sheep pen, and his renowned riding stables. He stopped short of bragging outright over the marvels of his ranch, but his glowing pride was poorly masked to a perceptive soul.

Jesus had said, *For it is easier for a camel to go through a needle's eye, than for a rich man to enter into the kingdom of God.* For some reason the words struck her, and she wondered if they had ever occurred to Joshua.

"Mr. Casey," she asked him, redirecting her thoughts to safer ground, "do you recall the day we first met?"

He smiled. "I remember how astonished you looked when I called you 'Ruby.' You'd think a man had never used your Christian name before."

She straightened her spine. "Never one I'd known for such a short acquaintance. At least not a *gentleman* I'd known for so brief a time."

He grinned, unrepentant, as Ruby went on.

"While we were at Mr. Morgen's house, we discussed the lack of a church in the valley."

More serious now, he nodded. "A sore lack."

"Yes. And it occurred to me—I know I'm new here and I often expect the impossible—but it occurred to me that if we had such a fine turn-out for a revival, surely most of those same folks would come to regular prayer meetings if we just had somebody to lead them."

He studied her gravely. "Maybe. But there are two problems, Ruby."

"Which are?"

"Well, first of all it's one thing to travel half a day for worship two or three times a year. It's something else altogether to do it every Sunday."

"We wouldn't have to do it every Sunday," she countered. "At least not to start with. Even once a month would be a beginning, Mr. Casey."

"That's true, Ruby. But it still doesn't solve our second problem. Our bigger problem, actually."

"Which is?"

"We don't have anyone to lead a formal prayer meeting."

Now Ruby faced him squarely. She'd been thinking of starting a church ever since the revival, and she'd decided that the best way to proceed was to appeal to Joshua's faith. And if that failed, to his pride.

"We have all sorts of people to lead it, Joshua. They just don't know it yet. Did Amos know he would become a prophet? Did Paul know he'd be writing half of the New Testament? Did Susanna Wesley know her cradle-rocking would produce a brand-new church?"

Joshua said nothing.

"My uncle leads us in prayer at home on Sundays, Joshua. He's good at organizing things, getting people together. That's important. His faith is strong but his voice is too soft to carry. You, on the other hand, have a power when you pray that could bring the hardest unbeliever to Christ," she told him sincerely. "Even if you couldn't handle a—well, an original sermon at first, you could read one of somebody else's!" She'd seen any number of fine books on the shelves in his study. "Or just read from the Bible. Half of these settlers can't even do that by themselves!"

Joshua was studying her carefully. No trace of humor remained on his face.

"And I'm . . . well, to be honest with you, Mr. Casey, my enthusiasm for music is a lot greater than my talent. But I've got my songbooks with me and I know the tunes of a hundred hymns by heart. If nobody else is willing to lead the singing, I'd give it my best."

Joshua took a deep breath and let it out slowly. He faced the meadow of Indian paintbrush past the stables and considered her words. "I never really thought it could be done before, Ruby. Not until we had a real town or at least a real preacher. But my mother's had me reading the Bible to her in the evening while she sewed ever since . . . well, ever since my brother died. I've made speeches once or twice when there was something that needed saying." He pondered her words for a long, quiet moment. "Maybe . . . maybe there is a way to start a church here after all." He met her eyes and smiled warmly. "I'll study on it, Ruby, and pray on it, too. Let's talk about it again after the barbecue."

Ruby felt so good she wanted to hug him, but she restrained herself. "Oh, thank you, Mr. Casey! I knew you were the one cut out for the Lord's work here!"

Their mutual smile embraced a special understanding that they had not shared before.

Quietly he asked her, "How long do we have to know each other before you can call me 'Joshua'?"

"I haven't figured that out exactly, Mr. Casey," Ruby answered with a grin, "but when I do, you'll certainly be the first to know."

"Howdy, friend! You must be Joshua's man, Morgen. I'm C.W. Warren. You're supposed to take me to the main house."

Wilhelm looked up from the harness he was fixing and glared at the greenhorn. He was very tall and slim, with smooth blond hair and regular features. His manner was pleasant enough, and, had Wilhelm been one of Joshua Casey's hired hands, he might not have been offended by the stranger's blithe assumption. As it was, there was no way to hide the fact that Joshua had conveyed to this man the impression that Wilhelm was not his social peer. It was equally obvious that Joshua had not given his neighbor the simple courtesy that Orville Barnett had extended when he was expecting kin. He'd never mentioned the fact that a tenderfoot might get off the stage just before dinner and demand a jitney to the *Rancho*.

"You are mistaken, sir," he declared firmly. "This is my land, and I work for no man." He could have added, *My grandfather was a Prussian serf, but I was born a free man as my father was before me. I did not fight my way out of a factory to do another rich man's bidding*. "Joshua Casey is one of my neighbors. You are half a day's ride from his ranch."

"Half a day's ride!" The man blurted out. "Why, I don't even have a horse. There's not even a road—"

"Should I call the horses, Papa?" Kelby interrupted, eager to lessen the signs of tension between his father and the stranger.

For a moment Wilhelm considered telling him no—Joshua's friend could walk to the *Rancho* for all he cared! That would teach the high and mighty Joshua Casey. But Christian neighborliness prevailed in the end. He nodded to his son, then turned to C.W. Warren.

"Be calm, sir," Wilhelm assured him. "I have been to the *Rancho* many times. I will take you in the wagon. You will be at your friend's house in time for supper." Wilhelm, of course, would not be back to his own adobe before dark; once more the cow would have to wait and Kelby would doze while bouncing in the wagon. Worse yet, the boy would have to spend the afternoon in the searing sun without benefit of shade. Somehow the cow had gotten hold of some yarrow the night before, and Kelby was still feeling a little sickly from the morning's tainted milk.

"That's right kind of you," the stranger assured him, totally unaware of all the conflicts in Wilhelm's mind. "I can't imagine how I made a mistake like that."

"Think no more of it," Wilhelm insisted. "I am sure that *you* are not the one who made the mistake."

All five of the Barnett women were busy whitewashing the house with Clara's home-made brew of lime and cactus juice when Kathleen saw the swirls of dust in the road.

"Company coming!" she hollered.

Phoebe frowned. "From the north side a th' valley. Wilhelm or the Jaspersons."

Ruby couldn't stifle the sense of elation that suddenly overtook her. In a matter of moments a drab and dreary day had taken on all the joy of Christmas. "I thought you liked Sarah Jasperson," she chided her cousin, trying to conceal how much she hoped the visitor was Wilhelm.

" 'Course I do. But Mojer's only eleven."

Ruby had been in the valley long enough to understand. Mo Junior was a fine boy, but in Phoebe's adolescent view, providing hospitality to any family without a man of marriageable age was a waste of time.

They all stood perfectly still in the yard, watching the road as the wagon approached.

"It's Wilhelm."

"Somebody go tell Reed 'at Kelby's comin'!

"He ain't alone."

"He's got a stranger with him!"

"Hedda's favorin' her right foreleg—prob'ly throwed a shoe."

Clara quickly assimilated all the information and made several quick domestic decisions. "Gonna have to stay fer supper now. Wilhelm's gonna be stubborn like always—we gotta make out like Kelby gonna starve if they don't eat with us. Even then ya know he's gonna make us take some food in trade, though th' good Lord knows he needs it more'n we do! The Morgens'll have ta go back home right quick 'cause a th' cow, but Orville can take this fella wherever he needs ta go on th' way ta Caytana tamarra. Go git supper goin', gal," she told her eldest daughter.

But Phoebe, for once in her life stone silent, stood transfixed as the wagon pulled into the yard. Her emerald eyes were on the tall blond stranger who bounced on the spring seat next to Wilhelm. She never heard a word the others said.

Ruby, on the other hand, heard all the conversation that went on around her in spite of her interest in the handsome but bewildered young man. She heard Wilhelm introduce the stranger and explain that this was the nearest ranch to the road where Hedda had thrown a shoe. She heard him question whether Orville should be put to the inconvenience of going out of his way to deliver Mr. Warren to Joshua. And finally she heard him vigorously deny that he was hungry and insist that Clara could only give food to Kelby or the stranger if she would accept one of his Poland China hogs as a gift in return.

Ignoring the grown-up negotiations, Kelby crawled off the wagon and bounced over to Ruby with a grin and a hug. His little face was so hot and flushed that not only did she give him a dipperful of water to drink, she poured a second one over his head before she took him inside the barn where it was cooler.

Ruby showed him Reed's new pinto pony in hopes that the two boys could go riding together now that her cousin had two horses the right size. She also wanted Kelby to see the new litter of pups born a fortnight ago to one of the sheepdogs. He was so entranced by the sights in the barn that he forgot to ask for Reed.

Eventually Ruby went back into the house to help Phoebe start the meal. But Susanna was helping her mother; Phoebe had volunteered to entertain their unexpected overnight guest. Kelby followed Ruby around the kitchen, insisting on playing with Reed underfoot when his friend finally caught up with him. Almost an hour of horseshoeing and man-talk passed outside before Ruby was greeted in the parlor by the big booming voice she had longed to hear for so many days.

"Good afternoon, *Fraülein*."

There were half a dozen other people in the house by then, but for the moment it was as though she and Wilhelm were all alone. Ruby didn't think about the tired gray broadcloth skirt she'd worn to whitewash the house; she didn't think about the myriad strands of ebony hair that had pulled loose from her wilted slate cap and feathered the widow's peak that crowned her lovely face. Her mahogany eyes sought his kind blue ones, sparkling with warmth for this very special man.

"It's good to see you, Mr. Morgen," she started off in a formal tone.

But Wilhelm didn't bother with preambles. "You are good to my son," he answered simply, as though there was nothing else that needed to be said.

Ruby braved an intimate glance in his direction, and in spite of the chaos in the kitchen, he gave her a smile that was almost as heartwarming as the one he'd offered her the first day they'd met. How rare the unexpected gift . . . how precious the honor from this unconventional giver!

Ruby didn't try to conceal the pleasure his friendliness kindled within her. She just stood there and grinned at him, dazzled by his radiant expression as he let her see his gratitude unmasked for ever so brief a moment. Then Clara and Susanna bustled pots and dishes out to the table; the door slammed and a gaggle of children surrounded them again.

"Ya sit yerself down, now, Wilhelm, an' no more talk about that hawg," Clara commanded. "I know you'd be more'n happy ta feed th' whole lota us if'n we showed up ta yer place unexpected-like."

Wilhelm stared at her, unmoving. Clara stared right back.

"Please sit down for supper, Mr. Morgen," Ruby declared in a soft but formal voice, hoping to end the stalemate. "I'm so glad you could join us for supper this evening."

Wilhelm turned to face her, mischief dancing in his eyes. "You are very kind, *Fraülein*," he replied, doing as she bid him without any further demur.

Clara harrumphed, but there was a smile on her round, wrinkled face. "Susanna, call th' resta them folks in here ta eat now," she bellowed to her daughter.

Wilhelm, the only one sitting at the big table, caught Ruby's eye and smothered a laugh.

Ol' Wilhelm ain't lookin' fer fun, Phoebe had told her. How little did Phoebe know about this complex man!

She grinned back before she set out the rest of the dishes, recalling how differently Joshua had behaved the day he'd joined the family for a meal. With sudden insight she realized that she wouldn't have minded in the least if Wilhelm had called her 'Ruby.'

Ruby was surprised by Cayetano. She'd been told it wasn't as big as Cincinnati, or even Los Angeles. But never in the furthest reaches of her heart had she expected a main street that took up less room than Joshua's horse barn and breaking corral!

Except for a handful of board and batten houses, there was only a dry goods store, a one-room schoolhouse, and a restaurant that had been built as an overnight stage stop. The crude adobe building still served as a hotel, but the family that ran it put folks up overnight more as a kindness than as a lucrative business. Likewise, their oversized barn served as a livery stable of sorts, and in the evening people gathered around the poplars that shaded the front porch.

"The school's too far away for us to send the young'uns," Uncle Orville told her, pushing his hat back on his head. "In the winter we teach them what we can. I know that's hard for you to understand, Ruby, but out here a girl can survive without learning to read as long as she can cook and sew. And a boy doesn't stand a prayer if he can't rope a steer or shoot to kill without reloading."

Ruby said nothing, but Phoebe chimed in with, "Ain't much of a school nohow, Ruby. The slates are made o' redwood bark an' they whittle down lead bullets fer pencils. Pa does us better'n that back home. Ellie Casey even got ta learn ta write on paper when she was little."

Orville helped the girls down from the wagon. "Someday we'll have a real school on our side of the valley. Maybe even in time for my grandchildren."

Much to Ruby's surprise, Phoebe blushed. She didn't even bother with her normal nay-saying about the valley's men. In fact, she hadn't had a single nasty thing to say about anybody since C.W. Warren had climbed down off Wilhelm's wagon in his wool sack suit and ruffled shirt. She'd chatted with him the whole evening and all the way over to the *Rancho* this morning on the way to Cayetano. Neither Ruby nor Orville had gotten in a single word edgewise.

"I'll go get Mrs. Kepler started on Ma's list," she told her father. "Come on, Ruby. We gotta pick out some darks fer Ma's piece bag. I can't believe ya left yer hope chest behind. Ain't nobody gonna get hitched up with ya out here if'n ya ain't got 'nuff quilts. Susanna's already got five an' Ma's workin' on Kathleen's second one already. Ya ain't got no time ta lose!"

Wincing at her cousin's well-meaning harangue, Ruby trailed Phoebe into the dimly lit store. Every kind of nail and harness and rope seemed to hang from the rafters; the shelves were full of bolts of calicos and barrels of flour. An open clay pot full of unwrapped peppermint sticks sat on the counter, right under a sign which read, "Fresh grizzly today: twenty cents a pound." A cuspidor dirtied the floor.

"Howdy, Mr. Kepler," Phoebe greeted the nearly bald gentleman in denim trousers and blue suspenders. "This here's my cousin. Where's yer wife taday?"

The old man turned slowly to study Phoebe, his face sad and drawn. "I reckon ya ain't heard yet, Phoebe. The missus has gone to her Maker. Cholera. Two weeks ago come Tuesday."

Ruby couldn't speak. Even Phoebe was utterly still. They were both familiar with cholera; they knew it could hit without warning and take its victim to heaven within a few hours. The body lost all fluids and simply ceased to function. Ruby had never met Mrs. Kepler, but the shock on Phoebe's face made the death seem almost personal.

"Mr. Kepler, sir, I don't rightly know what ta say," Phoebe finally mumbled. "'Ceptin' I am sa very sorry."

The whole town seemed to echo Phoebe's sentiment. Apparently Mrs. Kepler wasn't the only person who'd succumbed to cholera in recent weeks. Two ranchers far to the east had also died. The wife of one had been terribly ill but had recovered, as had two children on a neighboring ranch. And before Mr. Kepler finished loading Orville's wagon, a local man rode in with a body draped over a riderless horse—another victim of the terrible disease.

That night the Barnetts slept on lumpy straw-tick mattresses at the hotel; they left first thing in the morning. This time they took the more direct route through the north side of the valley since they didn't have to ride through the *Rancho*. Uncle Orville talked as they traveled, trying to broaden Ruby's appreciation of life in California.

"Gregory Kepler told me that a fellow just east of town is putting in twenty acres of walnuts, hoping to ship them to San Francisco by steamer until the railroad comes through. That's the sort of thing Wilhelm wants to do with his oranges."

Ruby's interest picked up. "I don't know too much about his situation," she admitted. "He seems to work awfully hard."

"He don't know how ta do nothin' else," was Phoebe's comment. "I ain't never seen him when he didn't look like he'd been rode hard an' put up wet."

"Man's carrying a mighty big load, Phoebe," her father reminded her. "He got off the ship with five cents in his pocket and a newborn baby in his arms. Took a job in a factory and paid a lady to care for Kelby 'til the shaver was old enough to make due without a woman tending him all day. I've got to admire Wilhelm. Anybody else would have given up long ago."

Before Phoebe could answer, Orville pulled up the wagon as he stared at the pathetic sight before him. A short distance from the side of the road stood the charred remains of a house and barn, black and broken beyond all hope. Orville sighed deeply and bowed his head.

"Dear Lord, have mercy on their souls," he whispered. Ruby and Phoebe added their own silent prayers. After a moment he clucked the team on.

"Do you know the folks who lived there, Uncle?" Ruby asked him.

"Yes." His voice was low and unsteady. "The Eversons. Good folks. Man, wife, three little ones so far. Heard in town they lost everything and went back to Colorado."

"Dry as a tinderbox this year," Phoebe remarked sympathetically. "Coulda happened ta anybody."

Orville shook his head. "I'm not so sure about that, Phoebe. It didn't happen to anybody; it happened to folks who lived next to the stage line that runs from Los Angeles to Cayetano."

Ruby didn't know what he meant by that, but the tone of his voice stroked her spine with icy fingers. Mr. Everson wasn't the only man in the sun-parched valley who owned land on the main road between Los Angeles and Cayetano.

So did Wilhelm Morgen.

It started out as a beautiful day. So beautiful, in fact, that Ruby could not bear to spend the morning inside.

"Aunt Clara," she asked just before breakfast, "is there any chance you could spare me for a little while this morning? I'd really like to take a walk before the sun gets any higher."

Busy with a kettle of hot water, Aunt Clara didn't turn around as she mumbled, "Too bad ya girls can't take a ride."

"Oh, why can't we, Aunt Clara? Surely you have a suitable mount for me."

Clara laughed. "What's yer idee of a 'suitable mount,' gal? One with velvet slippers on his hoofs and a neck bell that rings when ya need th' groom?"

Ruby was too hurt to respond. Instead she repeated, "Is it all right, then, if I go for a walk?"

Her aunt waved a fleshy arm. "Might as well. We could probably scare up a horse what wouldn't throw ya, but we ain't got no sidesaddle, gal. Out here if ya gotta ride a fella's horse, ya just git on and ride. I knowed one or two gals out here who wore men's breeches too, jist to make th' ridin' easier."

Ruby didn't know whether to be shocked or offended. "Aunt Clara, it's bad enough that Phoebe pokes fun at me all the time. Must you do it, too?" Uncle Orville's assurance that humor was the only cure for despair out here had not been much reassurance about the constant "rawhidin' " that Ruby had been subjected to. This was just another example. "I've heard of women riding astride, but I don't believe for a minute that any member of my father's family would stoop so low! As to women wearing trousers—"

She stopped at the look on her aunt's face. Incredulous. Hurt. Overwhelmed.

Ruby studied the wood plank floor and was suddenly grateful that it wasn't dirt like Wilhelm's.

"Ruby, gal," her aunt stated coldly, "yer a long, long way from Cincinnata. Out here we do what we gotta do ta get on with livin' an' keep from dyin'. We got no time fer fancy finaglin' or greenhorns who sashay inta this valley an' start tellin' us how they could do it better. Yer kin, gal, an' sometimes ya got a nice way about ya. We're all doin' our best ta make up fer ya losin' yer pa. But ya gotta learn that there's more ta life than talkin' purty over china teacups. There's times when ya put me ta mind o' Belinda Casey th' way folks say she was when she first come here!" she added in exasperation. "And there's times when I don't think she's changed none atall."

Dark red flooded Ruby's face. There was no graceful response, no courteous way to say she was sorry. Her aunt was right—and yet, so was Ruby! She'd been raised by certain standards, and even if it wasn't right to look down on folks who didn't have them, it wasn't right to disregard her own upbringing just because she'd landed in the wilderness. "You carry your values wherever you go," her father had always said. "It's who you are inside that counts."

"'Morning Ma, Ruby," Phoebe announced gaily as she sauntered into the kitchen, apparently oblivious to the strained atmosphere. "Fine day fer a picnic, don't ya think? If we took the young'uns outta yer hair, Ma, ya think me 'n' Ruby could take th' buckboard down ta th' crick?"

Ruby said nothing; she didn't know whether her cousin's suggestion was coincidental or intended as a salve to her own wounds. Aunt Clara, apparently more insightful than Ruby had given her credit for, nodded without looking at her niece. "Ask yer pa ta hitch up Jeb an' Brownie when he comes in ta eat. Don't know what trouble them two can get inta from here ta the crick."

Ruby decided not to ask who was going to drive the wagon.

Preparation for the morning's outing took more than an hour after the chores were done. By then the sun was high in the sky and Ruby was no longer sure she wanted to go anywhere with Phoebe, two chatty little girls and an incorrigibly wiggly boy. She wondered if Wilhelm ever took time off for a picnic. Surely he could respect the simple joy of a morning's stillness in a field of purple owl's clover, or a quiet moment by a running stream.

Much to Ruby's surprise, Phoebe was adept at handling a team of tired old horses. The wagon bounced over a little-traveled trail due west where it eventually intercepted what was left of the Sycamore River by this time of year.

They unloaded the basket of food and spread a tattered old quilt on the ground. "I wanna go swimmin'!" Reed announced.

"There ain't enough water in th' crick ta swim," Susanna informed him with the wisdom of her twelve and a half years. "When yer older Pa'll take ya up ta th' place where th' swallows nest on Manzanita Mountain. Hank an' Johnny swim there all th' time."

Ruby wasn't sure what the girl meant by "all the time;" except for the barn-raising and the revival, Hank hadn't left the ranch since she'd arrived.

"I don't know why Kelby couldn't come along," Reed whined as he munched on a piece of dried beef. "I don't never get ta see Kelby."

Neither do I, Ruby wanted to tell him. *Not to mention his father.* It troubled Ruby to realize that she was so aware of the slowness of time passing where Wilhelm was concerned. She hadn't the slightest idea when Joshua had last appeared or when he was due again, but she knew that precisely thirteen days had passed since Wilhelm had dropped by the ranch with C.W. Warren.

Ruby didn't want to think about Wilhelm; she was here to enjoy the scenery. In the deepest part of the creek a handful of reeds and bamboo grew under the willows like a tiny oasis of marshland in the middle of the arid grazing land that covered most of the valley. A clump of lemonadeberry bushes rose from the sumac and poison oak in the dry part of the creekbed, but other than that only star thistles and red-crowned buckthorn neck owned the barren ground.

"I know it ain't much, Ruby," Phoebe declared apologetically after the children trotted off to play, "but ya was hurtin' sa much fer a trip ta *somewheres*." The girl's tone was genuinely sympathetic. "Ma always says that it 'pears like just what a feller wants is what a feller can't have."

They shared a private smile before Phoebe stretched out on the quilt, her hands behind her neck as she studied the sky. "Come winter ya won't know this place, Ruby. We had a turrible flood two years ago an' th' crick went crazy. Grew three times its natural size an' then jist spilled over altogether. We lost purt near a hundred head a cattle that year. Now Pa says we're fixin' ta lose that many in th' drought."

"Drought?" Ruby asked. "This seasonal dryness isn't typical?"

Phoebe shot her an exasperated look. "It's a right hard summer, Ruby. Can't ya never talk like the resta us? Pa went ta school back there in Ahia, too, but he don't show off all the time talkin' up big."

Ruby didn't know what to say, so she tried the truth. "Phoebe, the way I talk is as natural for me as the way you talk is for you or Wilhelm's German accent is for him. I'm sorry if it offends you."

Phoebe shrugged. "Oh, it don't 'fend me. It don't even hurt my feelin's none." She grinned at her colloquial translation. "But what my ma said ta ya this mornin', cousin, well, I hate ta say it, but it's true. Ya never come right out an' say it, but we know yer lookin' down at us jist th' same."

Ruby was ashamed. No matter how hard she tried to hide her dismay for these simple people, her shock at their country ways and hayseed grammar, they would always know what was in her heart. In a way she was no better than Joshua Casey, who made no effort to conceal his disdain for the valley folks around him.

"Phoebe," she struggled to say, "I never meant to make you or your mother feel that I was well, looking down at you. It's just that everything here is new to me, and sometimes I can't hide my surprise."

The girl grinned and took Ruby's hand. For the first time Ruby felt as thought the two of them might really become friends. "It's okay, cousin. Ma always says, ain't none of us perfect." The grin widened. "Though I suspect that C.W. Warren comes mighty durn close."

Ruby laughed. "Is that what's happening to you, Phoebe? At first I thought you might be sweet on that young fellow, but when you didn't say anything. . . ."

Phoebe sat up and hugged her knees to her chest. "I know it's crazy, Ruby, but I knowed from th' minute I laid eyes on thet man, thet he was th' one fer me."

"Does he feel the same way?" Ruby asked gently.

Phoebe wiggled her fingers and shrugged. "I don't know, Ruby. He ain't been honeyfogglin' me more'n jist a little. I ain't never known a Frisco fella before, so I ain't sure."

Ruby studied her cousin quietly, carefully weighing her words. "Phoebe, are you sure that it's really C.W. himself you care about? I mean, if he were planning to homestead land here in the valley instead of managing a bank in Los Angeles . . . would you still want to get to know him better?"

Phoebe straightened and somehow matured before Ruby's eyes. "I'd marry him if he lived in Wilhelm Morgen's ugly little hut," she stated bluntly. "That's how sure I am, cousin."

Before Ruby could answer, a piercing wail devastated the afternoon stillness. A herd of thumping feet poured out of the lemonadeberry thicket in the dry riverbed, sounding to Ruby's terrified senses like far more than three small children.

"Phoebe! Help!" Reed screamed as he scrambled toward her, slamming into old Jeb as he careened toward his sister. "It's a bear!"

Ruby grew deadly still. Was this another joke on the city slicker? If so—

"Get in th' wagon! He's right behind Kathleen!" Susanna screeched as she hopped over the big wooden wheel and pulled the reins loose for Phoebe. "Grizzly!"

Phoebe needed no urging. She tossed Reed in the back and clambered up on the spring seat, knees and bloomers askew as she took hold of the reins. Expertly she backed the frightened team away from the river. They were turned around by the time Susanna grabbed onto her little sister's hand and pulled her into the wagon.

It was only then that the twelve-year-old realized that her grown-up cousin was still sitting on the frayed cotton quilt, literally paralyzed with fear. "Ruby!" she shouted. "He's comin'! We gotta go!"

Vaguely Ruby heard her, as if in a nightmare. She remembered the day she'd seen Wilhelm chasing Kelby, when the charging bear had turned out to be a gentle giant.

Susanna hopped out of the wagon and slapped

Ruby right across the face. Hard. She scarcely felt the child's hand. Her eyes were too full of the huge shaggy beast descending upon the clearing, roaring with rage at the small troop of humans fleeing before his wrath.

CHAPTER 7

WILHELM HAD NO USE FOR THE FOURTH OF JULY celebration at the *Rancho*. In the past he'd come to the annual event only for Kelby, who had so few childhood joys available to fill his days. But this year, Wilhelm had actually found himself looking forward to the holiday. With any luck at all, he might get to spend some time with the *Fraülein*.

At first the thought had alarmed him, but he'd reminded himself that his friendship with the young woman was simply that of new "immigrants" bonding for solace in a harsh and unforgiving land. It was not a relationship that could sully Oma's memory. Wilhelm had grown fond of the *Fraülein's* unpretentious smiles and quiet ways; she, in turn, seemed to understand him. Kelby, of course, adored her, and Kelby was as good a judge of character as a high-strung horse.

"Lookin' for anybody in particlar, Kelby?" Sarah Jasperson greeted the exuberant child with a grin as soon as the Morgens arrived. "Mojer's over back a th' barn playing ball with a stick. Couple a Caytana cousins are there too, so ya might git a real game goin'."

Kelby grinned and scrambled off before his father asked, "Is Reed here today? Kelby does not get to see him often."

"Reed is here, Wilhelm," she answered somberly.

He glanced up at her wrinkled, loving face, instantly alarmed. He knew Sarah very well, better than he knew any other woman in the valley. She was trying to tell him something.

"What is wrong, Mrs. Jasperson? Young Reed is not well?" It was always his first concern with people who mattered to him. Reed was not one of his favorite children, but the boy was Orville's child and Kelby's friend . . . and now the *Fraülein's* young cousin as well.

"He's fine, Wilhelm. All the Barnetts are fine. The young'uns had a run-in with that grizzly what hit Hansons' place again last month, but Phoebe got 'em all in th' buckboard an' kept th' team from spookin' long enough ta outrun th' bear. Ta hear Joshua tell it, Susanna was th' hero a th' day."

"Why is Joshua Casey telling this story?" Wilhelm asked, unaccountably irritated with the news. "If he was there, why did he not shoot the bear before it could frighten the children?"

Sarah shook her head. "He weren't there, Wilhelm."

"But he tells the story as though he were?"

"No." Her voice was low and kind. "He tells it as though it was his ta tell—on accounta because Phoebe's cousin was there."

He stared at her blankly. He understood the words she used, but he failed to comprehend their meaning. This sort of thing still happened to him occasionally. Usually he just feigned indifference; this time her words involved the *Fraülein* and a grizzly. He needed to understand.

"My English, Mrs. Jasperson. Sometimes—"

"They're keepin' company, Wilhelm. He's sparkin' her serious-like." To his surprise her words hit him like thundering rocks in a landslide. "Ever'-body in the valley seems ta know it 'cept fer you."

Ruby was enthralled by the Caseys' barbecue. It was a mixture of a midwestern barn dance, a Mexican fiesta, and a San Francisco ball at the height of the "season." Guests could choose from roast pork or beef or bullhead catfish fresh from the river. They watched daredevil *vaqueros* show their skill with a lariat while Joshua's mother kept her housekeeper running in circles with feather-light cakes and buttery crusted pies—not just apple but apricot and cherry in spite of the drought! And after dinner, while everyone was comfortably arranged among the pepper trees Harold Casey had imported for his wife to maintain the illusion of the cooler weather she'd grown up with, Joshua unveiled this year's surprise—a group of Chumash Indians performing music they'd learned at the old Santa Buenaventura Mission!

Ruby didn't really know what she'd expected them to look like; there hadn't been any tribes near Cincinnati for at least fifty years. All seven of the Chumash, nearly the last of their people, were in their seventies or eighties. They wore floursack shirts and baggy cotton breeches not unlike Wilhelm's. Like his boots, their moccasins were handsewn from deerhide. The leader of the group boasted a tattered black and gold vest that looked like it had once belonged to a prosperous Spaniard. It seemed to Ruby that except for their shoulder-length hair and prominent cheekbones, they didn't really look like Indians at all—just lonely old men waiting to die.

All of them sang, and several brandished drums. One played a flute ingeniously created out of an old rifle barrel. Ruby was hard pressed to describe the music, but it was inspired by some kind of religious chanting with a hint of a tune. At times it was eerie and haunting; at times uplifting and full of Grace. All of it reflected the awe and wonder these native converts had for the "Great Mystery"—their name for Ruby's God.

She thought of Wilhelm's need to pray in German and realized anew the majesty of faith proclaimed in all its holy ways.

"I'm having such a wonderful time, Joshua," Ruby told him sincerely as they shared an old porch swing a few hours later. Normally she wouldn't have sat so close to a man, but with so many people filling up every chair, sofa, and loveseat in and out of the house, she couldn't afford to be prudish. "I can't believe you planned this day with such care."

"Nothing is worth doing if it's not worth doing well," he quoted, pushing his foot against the yellow wooden porch to set the swing in motion. "I think you'll find that I also set out to achieve whatever task I undertake."

For some reason his words shadowed her bouyant mood. She'd tried to give him an honest compliment, but he'd turned it into a chance to pat himself on the back. He smiled as his mother approached, clad in a pale pink gown of beaded silk that couldn't have looked less appropriate for a California frontier gathering. Still, she looked lovely in a parchment sort of way. Ruby could see her fitting into any one of the neighbors' parlors back home, right along with the hand-tatted doilies and porcelain children's dolls.

They were beautiful, in their place. They did not belong in Sycamore Valley.

Phoebe had gushed breathlessly over the pink silk dress, lamenting her own new green calico which suddenly seemed quite inadequate for the occasion. But the moment that C.W. had ridden in, bouncing uncertainly on the Caseys' gentlest steed, Phoebe's face had "lit up like a June bug on a ripe strawberry," to quote her enthusiastic mother. Clara had been delighted to note that C.W., in turn, had looked "jist like a dyin' cowboy." For the first time it occurred to Ruby that maybe her cousin hadn't imagined that Joshua's friend returned her feelings. The two of them had sauntered off together, and Ruby hadn't seen hide nor hair of either one all day.

Joshua had greeted Ruby amiably, but his response to her own fitted yellow shirtwaist—generous with embroidery on the bodice and just the right hint of lace—had paled beside C.W.'s response to her cousin. "You look fine, Ruby," he'd decided after a brief appraisal. "Very appropriate for a Casey barbecue. Mother will be pleased."

Ruby didn't really care if Mrs. Casey approved of her new yellow dress, but she found herself hoping for a glance of approval from Wilhelm. But so far she hadn't managed to find him alone for an instant. Several times she'd gotten near enough to say hello, but before she could engage him in conversation he'd excused himself curtly or disappeared altogether. Granted she hadn't seen him for a long time, but their last evening together at Uncle Orville's had been so delightful that the change in his behavior made no sense to Ruby. She'd seen Joshua half a dozen times since then. Even though the picnic was at the *Rancho*, she'd hoped to spend most of the day with Wilhelm.

"Hello, dear," Mrs. Casey greeted Ruby primly as

she and Joshua continued to rock leisurely in the swing. "I do hope you're enjoying yourself."

"Yes, I—"

"Joshua, darling, Conchita needs a little direction regarding the meat. Do you think you could take care of it for me, please?"

"Of course, Mother," he agreed, his voice a shade softer than Ruby had ever heard it. She remembered the way he'd mentioned the woman in his noonday prayer last month and wondered why he treated her so tenderly. Was she secretly ill or was it possible that there was one person on earth whom Joshua truly cared for?

As soon as Joshua excused himself, Mrs. Casey gazed down at Ruby, then beyond her to the porch swing itself. "It's been a long time since I've seen a young lady in this porch swing with a Casey heir," she commented briskly. "Harold bought it just after we were married. He called it our 'sparkin' bench.' I missed riding in a carriage through the park in the City, so he thought we could pretend we were moving at a good trot in this swing!" She laughed, but there was no humor in her voice. "He did get me a splendid new carriage, of course, and half a dozen riding horses over the years. Always made sure my saddle was cleaned and ready. . . ." Her voice trailed off. Ruby was certain that Mrs. Casey had forgotten she was there.

For a moment she was gripped by a pang of sympathy for the proud, rich widow; she covered the other woman's mental journey with another compliment for her family. "I think Joshua must be a lot like his father. He certainly spares no time or expense to do something special for his friends."

"Don't be coy, dear," Mrs. Casey declared with sudden harshness. "You know perfectly well he's doing it up brown for you. Living out here puts a crimp in a man's style, but my son certainly does his best."

"Oh, I don't think the valley is any handicap to Joshua, Mrs. Casey," Ruby disagreed politely. "In fact, I think it has encouraged his creativity. Bringing in a Chumash Indian band is ten times more exciting than a traditional symphony! How thoughtful of him to remember how much I like music."

The other woman stared at her vaguely. Maybe she thought Ruby was crazy to enjoy the honest simplicity of the music the Indians had offered—in her mind, perhaps, their performance had been intended as some sort of comic oddity. But even if it had been toneless and devoid of rhythm, Ruby would have been touched by the fact that Joshua had tried to warm her life with song.

"Well, I'm glad you like it, dear. Joshua heard about them from his brother-in-law just before Christmas last year and paid quite a bit ahead of time to keep them in the area. I tried to talk him out of it, but he insisted that they'd be more entertaining than a monkey or a dancing bear."

Taken aback, Ruby shivered at the word *bear* before she asked, "You mean he had all this arranged before I moved here?"

"Oh, no, Ruby," the other woman assured her, completely misunderstanding her concern. "The only thing he'd arranged was the Indian band. The rodeo and the apricots from Los Angeles are new touches he added this year just for you, although he won't admit it even to his mother." She smiled ingratiatingly at Ruby before she disappeared. "I have to mingle now, dear. You know how that is."

Utterly deflated, Ruby abandoned the porch and set off in search of Kelby. Surely this was one friend who wouldn't turn on her today!

She found him in back of the barn, trailing Mojer

Jasperson like an eager puppy. Despite his obvious enjoyment of the game he was playing with the other boys, he charged toward Ruby the instant he saw her. His demonstrative hug filled her anew with love for the child, but she was humble enough to know that his affection wasn't just for Ruby, the person. Kelby was absolutely desperate for somebody to be his mother.

"I am tired of playing now, *Fraülein*. I do not yet know how to hit the rocks with the stick."

"It's easier with a real ball, Kelby. Where I come from, they have men who do nothing but play this game for a living, with a special horsehide ball and a hackberrywood stick called a bat."

His eyes grew big. "It is this same game?"

"It's still baseball."

"And it is . . . a whole town of men who do nothing but this?"

Ruby smiled. "It's not a town, exactly. It's more like . . . well, the group of *vaqueros* we saw today. But they all wear clothes that look the same, with bright red socks. They're called a team."

"*Team?*" He sounded out the word. "The men all answer to the same name?"

"No, they all have different names. But when they're all together they're called the Cincinnati Red Stockings, just like . . . well, like we all live in the Sycamore Valley, but your family name is Morgen, and mine is Barnett. We're all special people when we pray alone, but when we all praise God together, we are stronger yet."

Kelby stared at her for a moment. "I think you should tell me a different story today, *Fraülein* Ruby. This one I do not understand."

Ruby gave him a hug and led him to a cluster of shedding manzanita trees on the outskirts of the noisy gathering. One of the roots of a nearby liveoak was big enough for the two of them to sit on. They were deep in conversation when Wilhelm joined them half an hour later.

"You are never to wander off, Kelby," he growled at the boy. "For many minutes I have been looking for you."

"He didn't exactly wander off, Mr. Morgen." Ruby found herself defending Kelby with more defiance than she would have offered had Wilhelm not ignored her so blatantly today. "He was with the other boys until he came with me."

He did not respond to her explanation. "It is time to go. Now, *Kleines-Bärchen*." He mumbled something else in German, which surprised Ruby; he'd never deliberately shut her out of his conversation like that before. Suddenly she wished she'd studied German in school, just so she could better understand this man. Determined to hold him—determined to get to the bottom of this inexplicable new communication problem between them—Ruby asked a question that she'd pondered many times before. "I've often heard you call him *Kleines-Bärchen*, Mr. Morgen. What does it mean?"

"What I call my son does not concern you, *Fraülein*," he snapped. "Go say farewell to your friends, Kelby, while I saddle up the horses."

Kelby looked up at Ruby uncertainly, then hung his head. Reluctantly he left her side and headed toward the barn. His father also turned to go, but Ruby stopped him with a single word. "Wilhelm—"

She didn't mean to call him that, but in her heart she knew him by no other name. The instant the syllables were out of her mouth he swung around, eyes wide and startled.

"Please tell me what I've done to upset you," she begged him, the words flying from her mouth without restraint. "Please let me make it right. For Kelby's sake, if not my own."

At first Wilhelm did not answer. He did not look at Ruby; the soil beneath his feet seemed more inviting. At last he informed her tersely, "You have done nothing, *Fraülein*. It is time for me to go."

"No, Wilhelm!" Her own insistence surprised Ruby; so was her continued use of his Christian name. But suddenly it seemed too late to retreat to the old formality between them. "You've avoided me all day. I've seen you talk to Aunt Clara, to Belinda Casey . . . even to Joshua though you've got no use for him at all! Yet a dozen times you've turned away from me. It's bad enough that they're all laughing at me because of that terrible grizzly. I can't bear to have you mad at me, too!"

He glanced up sharply. "What terrible grizzly? The one little Susanna kept from harming you?"

Ruby did not meet his gaze. If Wilhelm laughed at her too, she would burst into tears. *Why?* she asked herself. *Why should I care if one more person laughs at me?* Phoebe had already told the bear story to anyone who would listen . . . and always at Ruby's expense. Wilhelm had always made it clear that he had no great use for friends. Why should it surprise Ruby that he had no need for her either?

She took refuge in formality. "I know you're anxious to be on your way, Mr. Morgen. I only wish to apologize for—whatever it is I have unwittingly done to offend you so greatly. I assure you that it was not intentional."

She started to march past him, but Wilhelm reached out to take her elbow before she took three steps. He had never touched her before when it was not absolutely necessary, and her intense reaction surprised her. A meadowlark song of hope and confusion filled her heart; the skin beneath his calloused fingers seemed to burn with the warmth of the sun.

"I will tell you the truth, *Fraülein*," he declared softly. "You will sit back down here for just a few moments, and I will tell you all of the truth. This I should have done before. I should have trusted you."

Confused but relieved that he was at least talking to her again, Ruby did as he asked. He moved over close to her side, looking down at her from his great height, but he did not touch her again as he spoke.

"My neighbor . . . my neighbor tells me that Joshua Casey is thinking to marry you. She says people who see me talking to you wonder if I am thinking the same thing. Because they think my son needs a mother. Always they think this. They try to find me a wife. They do not see that I am not thinking to marriage." He took a deep breath and plunged on. "So it is better not to be talking too much. More kind to you, *Fraülein*. Better that Joshua Casey should give you this fine house. So many things he has for you that I do not. Better that he not wonder how things are with you and me. Better for you not to wonder . . . or to wait."

Bravely he met her smoldering gaze. "I do not look to you for a wife, *Fraülein*. It is best that you should know this now—that you do not hope for what is not."

Ruby bolted upright, deep wells of hurt boiling over into fury as she lashed out at him. "So what have I possibly done to make you think I would want to marry *you*, Wilhelm Morgen? I want to marry a man who can fill my life with flowers and music and light—not pork and Prussian pride and just plain stubborness when it comes to friendly neighbors!"

She would have stalked off then, terrified that he would see her threatening tears. But Wilhelm moved quickly in front of her, blocking her escape. He tossed out one arm that would have encircled her waist if she'd taken another step forward. Suddenly Ruby wanted nothing more in this world than to feel the power of his embrace.

She froze. A tornado of feelings circled around them, shutting off the rest of the world. Ruby felt as though she were bleeding inside . . . and for some reason, she was certain that Wilhelm was bleeding, too.

"I am so sorry, *Fraülein*," he breathed against her temple. "I am sorry that I make things worse with my clumsy words. I wanted only for you to understand that you have done nothing to fill my heart with anger. Now it is I who have done this to you." She could almost feel the warmth of his bearded face so close to hers. "It is not *you* I do not want for a wife, *Fraülein*." His tone beseeched her to understand. "If this I wanted, you would not be . . . unpleasing . . . to a man. But I . . . I am like one already married, even though you cannot see my Oma." Finally he met her eyes. "I carry her . . . here." He laid his free hand on his chest and waited for Ruby to look there, too. "Do you see?"

Very slowly, Ruby nodded. This she could understand. Her father had never stopped being married to her mother, though he'd lived on for thirteen years after she died. In some ways the pain had eventually eased; in other ways, it had not.

A belated wave of embarrassment swept across Wilhelm's craggy features as he realized how much of himself he'd revealed. "Perhaps it is just as well for Oma not to live here," he rushed on to cover his feelings. "She was a sturdy woman like yourself, but maybe she also would have wanted a house with . . . 'music and flowers and light.' In Germany we had walls made of wood, not bricks of mud. And floors that kept out the winter rain."

"Oh, Wilhelm!" Ruby whispered. "I didn't mean to insult your house. It's a fine little—"

"She wanted me to make a cradle before we left, but always I was busy in the factory, working more and more hours, making money to come to America. She did not want to come, but she said, 'Husband, I will go where you want to be. This is your dream; we must make it so.' " He said the words with bitter self-reproach. "She thought I looked like a big bear also, like you did when we met, *Fraulein*. But she was never afraid of me."

"Wilhelm—"

"The baby . . . she wanted to name it after her father if it was a boy. 'A farm by the sweet water' means this name; a good name for a Morgen son. 'Ingrid' for a girl she wanted, to remember always her sister who died as a tiny one. But on the ship, you see, we did not know what it would be. She was so sick . . . we were all sick, sick with heartache for those we would never see again, sick to think we had lice for the first time in our lives . . . sick with feeling like animals locked in a cage or left in a boiling pot neglected on the fire."

For a minute Ruby thought he'd forgotten she was there, so deep was his immersion in the excruciating memory. And then he looked at her again and whispered, "So she called him 'Baby Bear,' the new life within her. Girl bear or boy bear, it did not matter. So much she loved him! So much she loved me. So still I call him this. You understand, *Fraülein*?"

Ruby didn't fully understand, but she nodded anyway. Desperate to soothe him, she lay one warm hand on his arm.

"*Kleines-Bärchen*," he repeated, answering the question she'd asked him twenty minutes ago. "*Kleines-Bärchen*, I still call him, *Fraülein* . . . to remember my Oma. It means 'Baby Bear.' "

CHAPTER 8

"I AM SORRY TO TROUBLE YOU, Mrs. Jasperson," Wilhelm greeted his neighbor at dawn the morning after the barbecue. Hedda held still for her tiny passenger, but Val snorted and pranced around the lady's yard. "There is something I must ask of you."

"Ya jist name it, Wilhelm," Sarah assured him, concern lining her aging face.

In all the years he'd lived in the valley, trading goods and services and friendly calls, Wilhelm had never asked a neighbor for a favor outright; it galled him to be doing it now. But there are times, his father had taught him, when a man must do what a man must do—even when it is neither safe nor prudent.

"I cannot take Kelby with me today, Mrs. Jasperson. This would be a good place for him to be."

The older woman smiled. "Ya know we'd love ta have him. He can help Mojer do his chores an' if he's real lucky, we might have one more stick a peppermint candy left from th' batch Mo brought back last week from Caytana!"

Wilhelm held the reins for Kelby as his son slid off the horse, then loosened her cinch as he'd been taught. He didn't do too badly for such a small boy on such a big horse. Wilhelm was grateful that at least one of his mares was gentle and patient with the tiny booted feet that stuck out halfway up her withers.

"I will return as soon as I am done," he promised Kelby, unable to hide the gravity in his voice. "I do not know how long it will be."

If Sarah was curious about Wilhelm's plans, she did not show it. She put her arms around Kelby, pressing his back against her legs as he wriggled to look up at his papa.

"We will be home in time to milk the cow?" he asked, his eyes large and troubled.

"*Ja, Kleines-Bärchen*. This I hope. You know I will never leave you for long," he added in German. He made it a point to speak English in front of his neighbors, but this was one of those moments when Kelby needed the private reassurance that only his native language could bring.

With a brief thank you to Mrs. Jasperson and a final nod to his son, he pressed his knees against the black mare's sides and turned her southward at a brisk trot.

The bear, they said, lived up on Manzanita Mountain.

It was cool and shady under the willows where Ruby and Joshua rested after dinner. Half a dozen deer had skittered off when they'd arrived in the Caseys' carriage at noon, and Phoebe had dislodged a raccoon family when she'd spread out her Double

Wedding Ring quilt over the shabby old one she'd brought along to this spot before. If she'd hoped to impress C.W. with her domestic skills, she'd succeeded; he'd spent the last hour praising her cooking, her sewing, and her charming good looks. But now he and Phoebe were strolling by the river, and the afternoon stillness was growing awesome in their absence. Ruby struggled for a way to fill the burgeoning silence.

"I can't get over how pretty the flowers are out here," she declared, studying the star-shaped yellow blooms on a clump of nearby wildflowers that she hadn't noticed on her last picnic by the river. "Even the summer weeds are lovely."

Joshua snorted. "Klammathweed is only lovely if you're not running cattle on your land," he informed her briskly. "In a drought like this it can do more damage to your herd than a marauding bear." He pondered his own words as he caught sight of two huge naked-necked condors hovering low to the south where Joe-David said the grizzly lived. "I think it's high time I sent my brother looking for that hairy old fellow. Shouldn't be too hard with that new repeating rifle; he's been hard pressed in the past with his old muzzle loader. You gals ran into that bruin near here, didn't you?"

His nonchalance amazed and irritated Ruby. When they'd first discussed this picnic, she'd been brave enough to mention her apprehension about returning to this spot, but Joshua had just laughed off her fears. "It's the only place in miles that's cool enough this time of year, Ruby. Never you mind about that nasty old bear. I'll take care of you."

For some reason Ruby wasn't particularly reassured. She'd been uneasy with Joshua ever since Wilhelm, of all people, had informed her that Joshua was seriously courting her. Belinda Casey's words had certainly confirmed that suspicion. Ruby couldn't help but be flattered that the most influential young man in the valley had more than a passing interest in her, but she wasn't yet certain just how she felt about him.

Certainly she didn't care for Joshua the way her cousin cared for his friend. Ruby couldn't imagine strolling with Joshua though a cluster of prickly pear cactus as though it were a city rose garden, actually holding hands in front of God and everybody after just a few weeks' acquaintance.

"Tell me, Mr. Casey," Ruby asked as nonchalantly as she dared, "Is this sort of . . . well, friendliness . . . common out here among spooners or is Phoebe just . . . well, a bit more outgoing than most?" Even though Orville and Clara had given her no particular directions regarding their daughter's demeanor during this outing, Ruby knew what they expected. She felt the responsibility keenly.

Joshua laughed as he always did—that rich, hearty tone that was too well-bred to be openly offensive, but too condescending to warm her on the inside. "Truly, Ruby, I think it's a little bit of both. I've seen things in San Francisco that would shock you, but much of what goes on in the valley would even surprise the folks in Los Angeles, and it's more or less a real town. It isn't really that people out here don't care for convention, it's just that . . . they can't really afford it."

"I don't see what holding hands and kissing has to do with where a body makes his home, Mr. Casey," she insisted.

He smiled with a gracenote of affection that she hadn't noticed in his expression before. It warmed her, somehow, even as it left her a bit unsettled. "Perhaps not. But let's take another example. Say—women riding astride."

Ruby was so appalled she could hardly look at him. "It's utterly indecent, Mr. Casey! In Cincinnati when a gentleman takes a lady on an afternoon ride, he doesn't expect her to leave her manners at the stable."

Again Joshua laughed, but he didn't look as jovial as he sounded. "My mother's words exactly! But Ruby, when a lady gets on a horse out here, it's generally not for a ride in the park. There's a steer stuck in the mud, or a man who's been bitten by a rattler, or a baby waiting to be born who needs a neighbor lady's help *right now*. Surely you've been here long enough to learn that just staying alive in California is pretty hard work at times."

Ruby knew he was right, but she still believed that there were certain standards a lady maintained wherever she happened to be. "If I ever have such an emergency, Mr. Casey, maybe I'll have to eat my words. But until then, I'm not about to climb up on any four-footed creature without a sidesaddle."

Joshua gave her a sidelong glance. "It just so happens that my mother has a fine one she hasn't used in years. I'm sure she'd be happy to loan it to you."

Memories of Belinda Casey still rankled. Ruby wasn't about to put herself in the other woman's debt. "You're very kind, Mr. Casey, but I don't think I could impose upon your mother. Besides, I don't really have any occasion to go riding."

He grinned. "That could certainly be remedied, Ruby."

She wasn't sure if it was the smile or the tone of his voice that stilled her protest; all she knew was that there was no graceful way to decline his invitation, and Joshua's kindness made her reluctant to wound him. Even if she'd actively disliked the man, his position in the valley—not to mention the fact that he was her uncle's closest neighbor and a very good friend—left her with limited options.

"Perhaps we can discuss this later," she suggested courteously, recalling with relief that they had planned to use this afternoon to lay the groundwork for the valley's first regular prayer meeting. "Right now I really think we should take a little time to discuss our plans for a church."

"You mean while the lovebirds are out of the way?"

Ruby had to smile. "You have to admit they're not likely to be of much help."

Joshua laughed out loud. It was one of the few times Ruby had heard him laugh that she didn't feel as though he were mocking her. "Ruby, I wish you could have seen C.W. the last time I was in San Francisco. His older brother had just been smitten by the cutest little heifer, and old C.W. just ragged him no end. Couldn't for the life of him see what use Nathaniel had for such a frilly creature!" Without warning, he met Ruby's eyes with a different look. "It's really quite surprising what can happen to a sane and sober man when he stumbles across the right woman."

Ruby shifted her position on the symbolic quilt and picked up her Bible as a hint that they should get down to business. She had almost grown accustomed to Joshua's flirting, but more than once this afternoon his tone had changed into something deeper, something more intimate than the kind of superficial words she'd heard from him before. His quiet intensity made her uneasy. She wasn't yet sure whether or not she liked the sensation.

"I take it you think that Phoebe may be the right woman for your friend?" she asked softly.

Taken aback, Joshua stood up as if to stretch his legs. "Doesn't matter what I think. C.W.'s already swallowed the bait—hook, line and sinker. I must say, though, that I'm a bit relieved."

"Relieved?"

"Yes, ma'am," he replied with a tip of his hat. "Quite relieved for at least two very good reasons."

"Which are?" Ruby was genuinely curious.

"Well, no offense intended, Ruby, but considering the way your aunt has been gunning for a husband for that girl, I'm mighty glad she's all sewed up—to a right fine man, and wealthy to boot," he tacked on rather belatedly. As he met Ruby's disapproving expression, he explained, "Ruby, don't look at me like that. Even Phoebe knows that she and I aren't at all suited."

Ruby didn't answer that. Instead, she prodded, "So what's the other reason you're glad she and C.W. are . . . getting acquainted?"

Joshua knelt back down to face her. Though he had never overtly touched her before, he reached out now to let one hand nest softly against her cheek. It surprised her, and she wasn't sure if she liked the feeling or not. "Like I said, Ruby, he's a right fine man—a wealthy man. That kind of competition I surely don't need." His voice was still controlled, but perceptibly softer. "I was afraid he might take a strong liking to some other member of Orville's family."

Ruby couldn't move. He was laying his cards out on the table, and it really was time to give him an answer—at least a hint as to whether or not he was wasting his time. Clara, of course, would have urged her niece to smile and give the man some encouragement—now that Phoebe had a wealthy beau of her own. Mrs. Casey probably would have suggested that she throw herself at his feet. But it bothered Ruby that the whole valley, including the man before her, expected her to be . . . well, not just pleased but *grateful*, somehow, that Joshua Casey had taken an interest in her. It never occurred to any of them that perhaps she didn't want him to come calling. Sometimes she wasn't even sure she liked the man! But he did deserve an answer. She struggled to give him one.

And then, inexplicably, the face of a different kind of man altogether was swimming there before her. A man whose face was weary with work and shadowed with pain. A man who could neither initiate flirtation nor recognize it in any guise. A man who had already made it painfully clear that he had not the slightest interest in the kind of relationship that handsome Joshua Casey was growing eager to pursue.

"Mr. Casey," she heard herself announce crisply, "I really think we should try to plan the first service before C.W. and Phoebe get back from their walk. I was thinking that Matthew 18:20 would be a good place to start."

Joshua pulled his hand back as though she'd slapped him. A welter of expressions crossed his face—a flash of anger, well-controlled—perhaps a smidgen of pain. But the dominant expression that Ruby read there was sheer disbelief.

Quite suddenly, she longed to hear the Lord's Prayer in German.

It was late afternoon and sweltering before he found the thirteen-inch track which proved he was on the trail of the grizzly. Val sniffed the air and neighed repeatedly, restless and uneasy. Wilhelm decided to tie her to the lone yucca that towered over the hillside lupines; it was tall enough to pass for a tree. He marched forward on foot for the next hour, cursing himself for wasting a whole day's work on a matter of honor.

He was no great shakes as a hunter; shooting one antelope out of a hundred bunched together was a sufficient challenge for Wilhelm. Besides, this grizzly should have been Orville's problem, or perhaps Joshua Casey's. The bear was marauding their ranches, killing their cattle, threatening their women. It was no concern of Wilhelm Morgen's.

At least, it should not have been his concern. And it had not been—for months now he had ignored the grizzly—until he'd heard what had happened to the *Fraülein*. It would have been bad enough if she had been a country girl, accustomed to the howls of owls at night and coyotes at dawn when they come in from the hunt. If she had known how to handle a horse when it was spooked by a dustdevil, or read the signs that danger lurked in the chaparral when all is hot and still. But for all her courage, the *Fraülein* knew none of these things. For all her brave silence as her cousin Phoebe had repeatedly gushed out her tale at the *Rancho*, Ruby had been terrified by the bear.

So engrossed was he in thoughts of the woman that he came on the grizzly with awesome suddenness. Fear pounded unannounced in the base of his chest. Still, he calmly lifted his cap-and-ball Hawken and fired across the clearing into the face of the snarling, silvertipped giant.

When the ball slammed into the bear's right ear, it reared up and roared, incensed with raw pain. Wilhelm jammed the ramrod back down the muzzle as the beast ripped across the meadow, ugly teeth bared as it challenged its assailant.

A second shot plugged the shaggy brown hump just before the bear reached him. Now there was no time to reload. All he could do was bang the butt of his gun against the grizzly's upturned snout as its massive paws thudded against his chest. It swayed but a minute, then ripped through Wilhelm's shirt in a single blow as it knocked him to the ground. Savage claws tore open his right leg as the pain blotted out all but the darkest of his thoughts.

Dear God, what will become of my son. . . .

It was Hank who brought home the sudden news that Mo Jasperson was dead.

"Fever got him, Paul Hanson said," Hank reported after a day's hunting on Manzanita Mountain with Paul's boy, Johnny. "Drove inta Caytana fer supplies a week ago. Hit him quick as a frog can catch a fly two days later. Funeral's tomorrow. Joshua's gonna pray over him."

The funeral was a painful occasion for Ruby, even though she'd met Mo Jasperson only a few times and barely remembered which friendly valley face belonged to him. But his death underscored the frailty of life in the west. It also brought great grief to those she cared about.

She knew that Wilhelm was Sarah's closest neighbor and he, of all people, would understand what she must be going through. But there was no sign of him at the funeral, and nobody seemed to know where he might be. Clara silenced Reed when he whined for Kelby, reminding him they had not come to the Jaspersons' to play. Taking her aunt's cue, Ruby chastised herself for thinking of Wilhelm at a time like this. Joshua was going to be the preacher, and that was all that mattered, wasn't it?

"Dear friends and loving neighbors," he began, his voice deep and strong, "we're gathered here today for the saddest of earthly occasions. One of our own has gone on without us. One of our own has been taken away."

He looked so regal in his ruffled shirt and black string tie. His carriage was that of a professional orator. Once Ruby had seen Rutherford B. Hayes speak in Cincinnati, and even standing on the back of a wagon on the edge of a half-harvested field of sweet corn, Joshua Casey had the former president whipped both ways from an ace.

But still his words troubled Ruby, as though the majesty of his delivery was more vital than the pain that must live in his heart. *It's just because I'm on the outside looking in that I'm seeing all this,* she told herself. *Forget the preacher; pray for the dead. And pray for dear old Sarah.*

They all prayed; they all helped to lay Mo Jasperson in the ground. His children clung to their mother, some silent, some in tears. Mojer was wearing a shirt that by its size must surely have been his father's. Ruby knew he'd taken over his father's role in the family as well. He was a whole year younger than Susanna.

"What's Sarah gonna do now?" Clara asked Orville on the way back home. "She can't run cattle alone with seven young'uns—though she might be brave enough ta try."

Orville pushed his hat far back on his head as he always did when he was thinking. "Joshua and I will be talking about that. Don't know as how I can buy the land, but I can help her out with the herd."

"When's Joshua comin' over?" Phoebe blurted out. "Like as not he'll be bringin' C.W. along, don't ya think?"

"Hush, gal," Clara barked. "A good man's gone. Can't ya give him a moment's peace 'fore ya start prattlin' on 'bout yer new beau?"

Phoebe pouted in silence for a moment, but Kathleen and Susanna started singing in the back, rocking in their chairs to the swaying motion of the wagon. Hank, who usually rode alongside the buckboard on his bay gelding, galloped on ahead as though to check the range. Reed crawled up the springboard seat and wedged himself between his parents.

"How come Kelby never come? Kelby likes Miz Jasperson. Me an' Mojer didn't git ta play none taday."

Orville and Clara exchanged a quiet glance before Phoebe grumped, "I bet ol' Wilhelm just didn't wanna take time off from workin' fer a man what's already daid."

Ruby couldn't help but reply to that. "I'm sure he had a better reason than that, Phoebe. Like as not he was afraid that Kelby might come down with something."

Instantly she regretted her words. All of them in the wagon—virtually everyone in the valley—had been exposed to whatever fatal disease had carried off Mo Jasperson. From the symptoms she'd heard Sarah whisper to Clara in hushed and anguished tones, she suspected that Mo had died of cholera.

Nobody was quite sure how cholera spread, but once an epidemic got started, there was no stopping it. It already had a firm grip on Cayetano, but Mo was the first victim on the east side of the valley. They could only hope he would be the last.

Still, Ruby wondered if fear of the illness was what had kept Wilhelm at home today. If he, like Mo Jasperson, ever got sick and died overnight, who would be the wiser? Who would take care of Kelby? And who would even think to let Ruby know? A vision of tiny Kelby filled her eyes; Kelby in his father's giant shirt and shapeless hat, staring vacantly down at a freshly dug grave as his buddy Mojer had done this morning.

A raw sense of danger burned in her heart like the poison of milkweed when it pierces the skin in the early spring.

All the way home Ruby fretted about Wilhelm. She could hardly ride over to his ranch to see if he and Kelby were all right; she didn't have a sidesaddle and she wasn't about to ask Phoebe to drive the wagon. The only member of the family she'd ever consider approaching for help was Uncle Orville, and chances were good that he'd only laugh at her—or see much more in her innocent concern than she wanted to reveal.

Still, she found herself hovering around the barn to talk to Orville as he unhitched the team. Hank was with him, of course, but soft-spoken Hank was not likely to repeat their conversation.

"Uncle Orville, do you . . . do you have any idea where Wilhelm might have been today?"

"Nope." He pulled off a leather strap. "None of my business where a man chooses to spend his time."

"Well, I know that, Uncle. It's just that Wilhelm is close to the Jaspersons, and if anybody would know how Sarah must be feeling—"

"I hate to disagree with you, honey, but Wilhelm isn't close to *anybody*. He works real hard to keep it that way. He feels out of place at most of our get-togethers. He probably just thought he'd be in the way."

While Ruby was considering that possibility, Hank surprised her by adding, "I don't imagine Wilhelm would like to think much about somebody dyin' and leavin' all those young'uns alone. Ain't been that long since his own wife passed over."

Her cousin's sensitive observation had some validity, but it still didn't erase Ruby's concern. "Be that as it may, I still think it's odd that he didn't come to the funeral. And nobody's seen him since the barbecue. If anything happened to Wilhelm, Kelby would be left out there all alone. And we'd have no way of knowing."

Uncle Orville straightened up then and looked her in the eye. "Ruby, sometimes we don't see hide nor hair of Wilhelm for months at a time. For that matter, we've got half a dozen neighbors strewn out over the north side of the valley that we don't see from fall to spring every year. I know it's hard to get used to, but that's the way life is out here."

There was a gentle note of laughter in his voice as Hank led the team away. "Don't you go mixing up missing the sight of a man with worrying about how he's getting on, Ruby. I think Wilhelm's doing just fine."

Ruby's face flushed as she hurried into the house. She avoided her uncle for the rest of the evening, but when she went to bed that night, her prayers were all for Wilhelm.

Phoebe was right. C.W. did ride over with Joshua to talk to Orville about Sarah Jasperson's cattle, even though the courageous lady had decided to stay on in the valley. But Phoebe hadn't predicted that the men would bring a third horse in tow. She was a small graceful roan, her red and white mane interwoven in a mixture that made Ruby think of an old woman's braided hair. She was gentle and friendly and came equipped with a freshly-oiled sidesaddle.

"I thought we might take a ride when I'm done talking business with Orville," Joshua stated matter-of-factly. "Unless you've got something better to do."

"I haven't been on a horse in a long time," Ruby told him, not sure what else to say. Her confidence had been shaken by her run-in with the bear; she wasn't even certain she could handle a horse anymore. "I can't say I've ever been much of a rider."

"Neither is my mother," he assured her with a

grin. "If she can handle Promise, I'm sure that you can."

Ruby didn't want to look at him. "That's an interesting name."

"My father chose it. He said he'd buy her a special mount if she'd promise to go riding with him every morning for the rest of her life."

"Did she?"

He didn't answer right away. He gazed at Ruby intently before he answered, "Yes. But Pa died about a year after he bought the mare."

He made the announcement matter-of-factly, but Ruby wondered how deeply his father's passing had affected him. "You . . . had to take over then, didn't you, Joshua? Just like Mojer Jasperson."

For just a minute Ruby wondered if he'd let down the shutters and allowed her a glimpse of the real Joshua Casey—the one who lived beneath the pearl cuff links and hand-tooled boots. It was a futile hope. "Hardly," he replied briskly. "I was twenty-three and already privy to all aspects of my father's financial affairs. Joe-David would have had a harder time. He knows cattle inside and out, but dollars and cents on paper . . . well, that's something else altogether."

Somehow Ruby was disappointed. He could have used this opportunity to show her his heart, and instead he'd puffed out his chest just a little bit farther.

For no particular reason she wondered if Wilhelm's father was still alive and whether or not he had younger brothers left in Germany. She also wondered, as she had every hour for the last three days, whether or not Wilhelm was all right.

"Have you been back to see Sarah since the funeral?" she asked. "Or talked to anybody from over there?"

"No. I told her I'd talk to Orville and my—" He stopped and gave her a hard look. "I've got no other close friends on that side of the valley, Ruby. Do you?"

Suddenly she felt as she had her first day in that awful stagecoach—swamped by the loneliness, overwhelmed by the sense of being out of step with everyone she met in the valley. Only Wilhelm and her uncle really understood anything about Ruby, and Wilhelm, it now appeared, wanted as little to do with her as possible. Orville cared deeply for his niece, but he was too busy to spend much time coddling her emptiness and insecurity, especially with a well-heeled catch like Joshua Casey hovering about.

"There are times," she said simply, "when I'm not sure I've got close friends on this side, either."

For a moment they stared each other down. Ruby was too hurt and angry to care if Joshua rode off with his fancy roan mare and she never saw him again. It seemed to Ruby that he, on the other hand, didn't know how to be hurt. Even anger was something he kept well hidden.

Incredibly, it was Joshua who backed down this time. "I'm sorry, Ruby," he managed to force out. "I had no call to say that."

Ruby bowed her head in silent acquiescence, waiting for him to go on.

"The simple truth is, I'm not used to working very hard to . . . gain a lady's interest. I guess I am . . . confused by your actions sometimes and quite frankly—" he struggled for honesty, "—when I see you defending that stubborn dirt farmer, I'm more than a little bit jealous."

It was out now; he'd finally said it. Ruby could have told him that his jealousy was a waste of time. Wilhelm didn't want her; she was doing her best to turn her heart elsewhere. Still, she was not about to let Joshua Casey dictate her social life.

"I see no reason why any man ought to tell me who my friends should be, Mr. Casey," she stated clearly.

He heaved an exasperated sigh, then nodded once, relenting. When he spoke, his voice changed again—to that gentle, intimate tone she'd heard on the picnic—as he asked her, "Would you care to go riding with me today, *Miss* Barnett? I'd be much obliged."

And Ruby, hoping to put Wilhelm out of her mind once and for all, responded quite deliberately, "I'd be delighted, *Joshua*. Just let me get my bonnet."

"C.W. didn't say nothin' 'fore he left, Ruby!" Phoebe whispered mournfully as she curled up in bed that night. "He didn't say he'd be back fer me. He didn't even say he loved me. He's goin' to Las Anglas forever an' ever! What am I gonna do?"

Ruby didn't know what to tell her. Her own thoughts were full of the two men who seemed to be crowding into her daily life—Wilhelm by his absence, Joshua by his demanding presence. But she'd had years to grow accustomed to waiting, and she wasn't in the first throes of undying calf love like her cousin. Personally, she thought C.W. had made the right decision to leave Phoebe without making a promise he might later regret. He hadn't known her very long, after all. Besides, she was only sixteen.

But Ruby couldn't say any of this to Phoebe. "He's got a big new job to do, Phoebe. His family is counting on him. Maybe he's just not free to be thinking about a bride yet."

To Ruby's surprise, her frivolous cousin suddenly burst into tears. It was the first time she'd ever seen Phoebe cry. "I don't wanna rush him none, Ruby.

I'll wait jist as long as it takes. I jist wanna *know*, don't ya see? I'll keep waitin' anyhow, but if'n he'd jist a tol' me—"

Ruby knew just how Phoebe felt. Nothing in this world was worse than not knowing—decisions unmade, questions unanswered.

"Phoebe," she suggested gently, "do you think you'd feel better if you prayed? You know that the Lord has the final say in this, and He'll do what's right for you. If you're meant to live out your earthly years with C.W. Warren, that's surely what will come to pass."

Phoebe sniffed a few times, then nodded. "You say it, Ruby. You and Joshua are good at that. You do the prayin' an' I'll say it in my heart."

Ruby wasn't sure how good she was at public prayer; she and Joshua had decided that he'd do the talking next Sunday and she'd lead the songs. But she knelt down with Phoebe and prayed just the same—for C.W.'s safety and Phoebe's peace of mind. And then, as she had every day since the funeral, she added earnestly, "And please watch over Kelby and Wilhelm, Lord, and help me to believe that all is well with them. Amen."

Phoebe opened her eyes and stopped crying. "You're still worried about that funny ol' guy? With Joshua Casey all but beggin' ya on bended knee?"

Ruby shot her an impatient glance. "You don't have to like Wilhelm, Phoebe, but if you had any inkling of what makes him tick, you'd realize that he'd never miss Mo's funeral without a terribly good reason."

For a minute Phoebe just stared at Ruby before she lowered her eyes and whispered, "I know. Scares me some, cousin."

Despite the muggy summer night, a chill gripped Ruby's bones.

CHAPTER 9

ELEVEN WAGONS, ONE FINE CARRIAGE, and almost twenty saddle horses clogged the stagecoach road to the Tree by the time the Barnetts arrived on Sunday morning. Joshua met their wagon and helped Ruby down first, then politely assisted each of her cousins, sparing a smile for the lovesick Phoebe.

"He'll be back some day, Phoebe. I'm sure of it," he assured her gently when he saw the tears in her eyes. "I know him like a brother, girl. You're the one he wants."

To Ruby's surprise, Phoebe threw her arms around Joshua's neck and gave him a quick hug before she disappeared into the crowd.

"I hope that's contagious," he told Ruby with a grin. He waited for some sort of greeting, but Ruby's eyes were combing the assembled families. "*Ruby*," he repeated impatiently after a minute, "would you mind saying 'hello'?"

Belatedly she met his eyes. "I'm sorry, Joshua. Hello. It's good to see you."

Still he stared at her.

"I—I was looking for someone."

Joshua took a quick glance toward the base of the Tree. "He's right over there."

Ruby was too elated to worry about Joshua's feelings as she swung her eyes in the direction of his quick nod. If Wilhelm was here, in any condition at all, then her fears had been groundless! Relief soared through her as she spotted him leaning casually against the trunk of the Tree, Mojer Jasperson by his side. Both were turned toward the trickle of mossy water where Kelby leapfrogged over the stones.

It took a minute for Ruby's heart to cease its ponderous thudding. Wilhelm looked . . . well, he looked like Wilhelm. Shaggy in spite of his freshly combed hair, mussy in spite of his cleanest old shirt. Of course she was only looking at the back of his head, but still—

"Why don't you go on over and say howdy, Ruby. I'd like to have your attention sometime before we start the service."

Ruby was startled at the sound of Joshua's voice; more startled yet at the look of genuine frustration, if not despair, that colored his handsome face. Was it really so obvious? She could have told Joshua the reason for her preoccupation with Wilhelm this morning, but she doubted that he'd believe her. Besides, it was hard to put credence in any of her concerns while the sun shone and Kelby giggled by the stream.

"I'm sorry, Joshua. I didn't mean to be inattentive. I simply . . . I had something on my mind." She gave him a glowing smile. Then she looked at him, really looked at him, and her smile widened.

He was wearing a new black suit she hadn't seen before, with light stripes and wide lapels and a silk shirt that rustled when he moved. He was truly a dashing figure of a man. Ruby could see why he found it hard to understand her interest in a man who looked like Wilhelm.

"Why, Mr. Casey, you certainly do look the part today. I believe you could turn the head of every fine lady in Cincinnati."

He smiled back a little cautiously. "Just one head would be enough for me, Miss Barnett. And may I say that you look pretty as a picture yourself."

Ruby yielded to his engaging grin and took the arm he offered. She knew that even in her best pink linen shirtwaist, she looked wholesome and fresh-scrubbed rather than irresistible. But she felt pretty under Joshua's warm gaze, and it was a feeling she couldn't measure in dollars and cents.

"Could you all gather round over here?" Orville was beckoning to the group, indicating the loosely clustered chairs they'd all brought along from home. The people moved slowly, continuing to greet each other as they threaded their way through the food baskets and milling children. Some of the men and older boys chose to perch up on the wagons, boots dangling against the wooden spokes of the high wheels. "I know that some of you have wanted to start a church out here for a long time. Well, my dear niece and Joshua Casey have decided to do something about it!"

Everybody clapped, and one old grandpa called out, "I hear that's not all they've decided!"

Joshua smiled, working the crowd as he led Ruby up to Orville's side. She found three straightbacked chairs there—one for her, one for Joshua, and one for her stack of hymnals and the family Bible. After she was seated, Joshua stood up and faced the group.

"I'm not a preacher," he began. Good-naturedly they booed him down.

"Best one I ever heard!" somebody called out.

"Coulda been if you'd a mind fer it!"

"Read us a chapter, Joshua!" his mother coached from the sidelines.

Joshua waved them into silence and started again. "I'm not a preacher, but Ruby here knows a lot about church music. Back in Cincinnati, where she comes from, she was in charge of the singing and playing the piano, so she knows more about the right way to set up a prayer meeting than I do."

This announcement was met by a spattering of applause, less vocal than the offering for Joshua. Ruby didn't expect any praise, so she couldn't understand her instinctive need to search out Wilhelm's eyes in the congregation. It was the first time since Joshua started speaking that she'd let her attention wander. Now, spying Wilhelm, her thoughts moved quickly away from the man in the handsome new suit.

There was something wrong with Wilhelm. She couldn't put her finger on it, but there was something wrong. He was facing Ruby, but his blue eyes were dully trained on Joshua. Not with a smile or a glance did he seek to encourage her. His face had a gaunt, shadowed look that the heavy growth of red beard could not hide. Stranger still was the fact that he was sitting on a chair that wasn't his, while a woman twice his age stood behind him, looking more than a little bit weary. Kelby sat at his feet, tracing circles around the katydid in the dirt. While his small son's behavior was not bad enough to attract much attention, it wasn't like Wilhelm to allow Kelby such latitude in matters of deference to adults or reverence to God.

"So Ruby's going to start us off with the first hymn," she suddenly heard Joshua say—and wondered how many times he'd already had to say it.

She flashed a quick smile to the group and whispered a prayer in her heart. *Don't let me fail in this endeavor, Lord. Lift me up to sing your praises. Help me start a house of worship in your name. Guide Joshua in his first real sermon. Hold us in your mighty hand.* She wished her father could have been there, praying right beside her. But she was sustained by the faith he had taught his only child.

Nervously she opened her *Select Songs of Praise* to Hymn Number 141 and began to sing the only song that could have given her the strength to risk failure in front of so many people.

All hail the power of Jesus' name,
Let angels prostrate fall;
Bring forth the royal diadem,
And crown Him Lord of all;
Bring forth the royal diadem;
And crown Him Lord of all!

Ruby's voice was unsteady on the first few words, but a lifetime of singing those heavenly notes made each one fall in place for her. The people gathered in His name listened uncertainly at first, but when Joshua joined her on the second verse, they began to echo her words, in faith and joyous memory of hundreds of Sunday mornings not so very different from this one. And by the time she reached the fourth verse, which spoke of "every kindred, every tribe on this terrestrial ball," she heard a new voice struggling with the a capella notes. A voice that was clumsy and tone deaf and new to the song and the English tongue, but long acquainted with the grace of God.

Wilhelm Morgen was singing.

From that point on, Ruby's heart began to soar.

The songs were awkward, of course, with only one hymnal for so many souls with a mixture of religious backgrounds and vocal talents. And some of the folks, admittedly, had only come because they had so few chances to mingle with their neighbors. But overall the group exuded a sense of reverence, especially when Joshua preached on forgiveness of one's neighbors and the need for a church community in the valley. He quoted heavily from the book of Matthew, and nobody who heard him, least of all Ruby, could deny that he was a powerful messenger for the Word. By the time the service was over, she felt a kinship with Joshua that she had never felt before. Their labor of love, this first awkward worship under the boughs of the sycamore Tree, was but the first notch on the bottom log of the valley's future house of God. But they'd taken that first step together, hand in hand, and they were proud of themselves and grateful to serve the Lord.

If Wilhelm was also proud of Ruby, he was not about to show it. He only moved from his chair once, and that was to usher Kelby to a spot at the Jaspersons' dinner table. He made no attempt to look for Ruby or even acknowledge her presence. Joshua, on the other hand, made it very clear to everyone that the Barnetts and the Caseys were sitting together, and Ruby's place was next to *him*.

She sat with Joshua and smiled at his friends, accepting praise for her singing and agreeing with everyone's acclaim of Joshua's preaching. To no one's surprise, his mother was his most vocal aficionado.

"Ah, he could have been a preacher if his father hadn't died before he finished school," she told everyone within hearing distance, ignoring the fact that he'd studied journalism and still cherished dreams of starting a valley newspaper. "What a waste! A voice like that! He could have been a congressman or a doctor or a banker like C.W! But here he is . . ."

Clara, off to Ruby's left, snorted unceremoniously in her ear. "I know that ev'ry crow thinks his is th' blackest, but my how she do go on!"

Ruby stifled a laugh and turned her gaze back to Wilhelm. He'd finished dessert and followed Kelby off toward the river, where he and some other young tadpoles were busy trying to catch speckled trout with their bare hands. It was the only time since she'd arrived that Ruby had found Wilhelm alone. Slowly, unobtrusively, she excused herself and edged toward the Tree.

Behind her she heard the rattle of crockery and washtins as the women started cleaning up; she knew she ought to be helping them. But surely she could spare a moment to greet a neighbor, to spare a hug for his child? Yet it didn't seem to be her decision. Wilhelm didn't notice she was there.

Unlike that miserable encounter at the *Rancho*, this time Ruby didn't take his behavior personally. She was more certain than ever that something terrible had happened to Wilhelm. When he limped toward the river and called his son with complete disregard for the happy sport in which Kelby was engaging, she was sure of it.

She watched surreptiously from her spot near the Tree as father and son made their way toward the adobe without telling anyone goodbye. The instant they were safely out of view of any but the most determined observer, Wilhelm released the boy's hand and feverently clutched his small shoulder. His right leg began to drag as he leaned heavily against little Kelby. His right arm dangled uselessly by his side.

Fear for Wilhelm surged through Ruby like a shaft of lightning, along with shame that she'd let her pride overrule her instinctive perception that Kelby had needed her help. Propriety warred with emotion for just a second. Then she skirted the clearing beneath the Tree and hurried down the path that led to Wilhelm's house.

Kelby answered the door to the sound of her voice before his father could bark out gruff orders for the boy to wait. Ruby slipped inside just in time to find Wilhelm hunched over the bed, struggling to pull his boots back on before she saw him.

"Don't move, Wilhelm," she commanded. "I know you're hurt, so don't waste my time pretending. I've done my share of nursing and I'm not leaving this house until I've heard the whole story and treated your wounds."

Though his face looked pinched and white, for just a moment he looked proud enough to fight her. And then, incredibly, he slumped back down on the bed.

Nothing could have frightened her more.

"Have you had any fever?" she asked bluntly, determined to conceal her feelings. "Any sign of infection?"

He sighed and studied the ceiling. "The fever is gone now, and so is the bleeding and the pus," he admitted slowly. "The worst is over, *Fraülein*. Three days ago I could not have walked to the Tree."

"I had to help him get to the barn," Kelby chirped up. "I fed the chickens and gave water to the horses, but I could not milk the cow. Papa tried to show me but—" he held up a grimy hand in front of Ruby and flexed his tiny fingers "—I am not so strong."

Ruby was so angry she could hardly speak. Stubborn, stubborn man! With so many neighbors who would have been glad to help him! "Kelby, can you go fill the kettle with water? I need to wash off your papa's wounds."

Wilhelm shook his head as the boy scampered off. "You do not need to do anything. Once or twice I have changed the dressings."

"On your right shoulder? How could you possibly do that by yourself?"

He didn't answer, but he did not fight her as she bent over him and unbuttoned his shirt. The sight it concealed did not surprise her. The awkwardly wrapped rags, once clean, were now soaked with blood, but none of it was fresh. As she peeled off the bands she saw no lingering signs of infection, but the long, deep gouges that had caused it were unmistakable. Ruby couldn't tell if they'd been made by an animal's heavy claws or the iron spikes of a pitchfork or rake. She was not about to ask.

"How about the leg?" she questioned him.

He shrugged. "About the same. Worse it hurts when I walk on it."

She didn't even dignify that comment with a response. Refusing to be prissy about his clothing under the circumstances, she lifted the dusty butternut broadcloth enough to see more rags, more blood . . . and more deep gouges. These were not as deep, but covered a longer expanse of skin. Surely they'd been carved by some savage animal. Bear, bobcat, mountain lion? Ruby had no way of knowing.

She pulled off Wilhelm's sock and started to unwind the rags just as Kelby returned with the water. She wanted to shield the boy's eyes from the angry red sores on his father's body, but she realized that he'd already seen them more than once. Surely he'd helped his father bandage his shoulder.

New fury welled up inside her as she gathered kindling for a fire. Considering the heat of the day it seemed ridiculous, but she needed to wash out the rags as well as the wounds. There was no sign or smell of gangrene, but the risk of infection was still great.

"Come here, Kelby," she told the small boy, eager to give him some attention so Wilhelm could rest. "Would you like me to tell you a story?"

"Oh, yes, *Fraülein* Ruby!" he responded eagerly, quickly assuming his usual spot on her lap. "Can I hear the one about the big boat again?"

Ruby thought a minute. "Not this time, Kelby. There is another story that Jesus told about a man who helped a stranger he found lying hurt by the side of the road. I'm sure you'll like it." She gave the boy a quick hug and launched into the story while the water laboriously moved toward a boil.

For the next half hour Wilhelm did not move. Ruby tended his son, washed his bandages and cleaned his wounds. She tore up an old pillowslip to bind his leg and shoulder, her hands calm and firm while her face was stiff and hot. She knew she needed to hurry; sooner or later, someone would notice her absence. If Joshua realized where she'd gone he would be furious, regardless of the circumstances. Ruby knew he had no right to question her whereabouts, but she had no desire to upset him today.

Only when Kelby left to carry the dirty washtin outside did Wilhelm speak again. "I have never seen you so angry, *Fraülein*. I am sorry to have made you unhappy again."

"Unhappy!" she barked, suddenly unable to refrain from speaking her mind. "I am outraged! How could you be too proud to let anyone know you needed help. Milking the cow, indeed! You stomped around the service today and didn't even let us pray for you, let alone tell us you were in trouble. For all I know you've been lying here in pain ever since Mo died!" She glared at him. "Have you?"

He could not meet her eyes. "It does not matter."

"Maybe it doesn't matter to you, Wilhelm. Maybe you don't care if you collapse and die here all by yourself. But doesn't Kelby mean anything to you?"

Suddenly he faced her, his blue eyes dark and tense. "My son," he whispered dangerously, "means everything to me, *Fraülein*. This you surely know."

Triumphant that she'd found a soft spot, Ruby pressed her point home. "Then think of him, Wilhelm! What would he do without you? The nearest ranch is miles from here and—"

"I have taught him how to get there on a horse. He knows what to do."

Ruby shook her head. "He's only a baby. He should be allowed to be a child. But you've made him grow up before his time, Wilhelm. You've let pride get the better part of love, and that little boy is the one who's going to pay the price. For the rest of his life!"

Kelby walked in on the last note. The bright smile on his darling face faded as he studied the tense faces of the two grownups he loved best in the world. Nervously he suggested, "Always you tell to me a story, *Fraülein*. You will feel better if I tell to you a story before you go? *Ja?*"

His earnest plea touched Ruby. She was angry with Wilhelm and worried about the time, but she knew if she stomped out now, little Kelby would be the one to feel her wrath. His father was surely immune.

"That would be very nice, Kelby. You can tell me one short story before I go back to my uncle."

Kelby grinned, relieved, as he took Ruby's hand and led her back to the table. He pushed her gently into a chair and then scrambled up on her lap. "This is a true story, *Fraülein*, even though Jesus did not tell it. It is about a giant, humpy-backed bear and a very brave man who went out one day to hunt it down."

"Oh?" Ruby asked cautiously, her eyes slowly meeting Wilhelm's. "He did not go all alone, did he?"

"Yes, he did!" Kelby told her proudly, failing to hear his father's parched reprimand. "He is the bravest man in the whole world!"

And the stubbornest, Ruby thought to herself. "Tell me, Kelby," she continued, "Why did he go out to hunt the bear alone? If it was bothering his animals, why didn't he ask the others to help him track it down?"

"But he did, *Fraülein*. The other men all talked about it, but they never did a thing. So—"

"Kelby, that's enough," Wilhelm whispered hoarsely. "The *Fraülein* does not want to hear about the bear."

Kelby hung his head, all vigor suddenly depleted. "I am sorry, Papa. I only wanted to make *Fraülein* Ruby feel better."

"I know, *Kleines-Bärchen*," Wilhelm told the boy more gently. "But it is not good to boast to one's neighbors about one's own family. Besides, the *Fraülein* will be missed if she does not soon return to the Tree."

So I am dismissed, Ruby thought resentfully. *And once I worried about sounding condescending to this man*. Forcing her distress deep into the hidden reaches of her heart, she gave Kelby an extra big hug before she stood up and set him on the ground. "I hope I'll see you soon, Kelby." Her eyes met Wilhelm's quickly. "You take care, Wilhelm," she managed to say.

Briskly she strode toward the door. Before she

could open it, Wilhelm's voice, low and strained, arrested her proud flight.

"*Fraülein?*"

"Yes?" She did not turn around.

"You did not ask, but the bear—the bear is dead."

Slowly she pivoted to meet his eyes. She could not mask her relief. "I'm so glad to hear it, Wilhelm. To have him so close to Kelby—"

"Close to Kelby?" he asked her, puzzled. "I would never let him close to my family!"

Ruby stared at him. "I didn't mean that the grizzly had moved into your house, Wilhelm. But I'd only heard that he'd been sighted on our side of the valley. If you found him on your land—"

"I did not find him on my land, *Fraülein*. I tracked him from the southern tip of your uncle's ranch and found him high on Manzanita Mountain."

Ruby could not conceal her exasperation. "Why, Wilhelm? Why on earth would you risk your life to track down a bear on the other side of the valley? You're not the kind of man who has to prove to the world how tough and strong you are."

Before Wilhelm could answer, little Kelby thrust himself before his father and implored Ruby with his bright blue eyes. "Oh, please do not be mad at my Papa, *Fraülein*! Do you not know that he did it for you?"

Ruby could make no sense of the child's words. "For me?"

"Yes!" Kelby insisted. "After the barbecue he prayed for your safety until he could find the grizzly. I heard him tell God that he could never bear to look into your eyes and see fear there again."

The starch melted from Ruby's spine as she stood there before the two of them—embarrassed father, proud little son. She couldn't for the life of her think of a word to say. Perhaps, by coming here under these conditions, she'd already said it all.

"Kelby, walk the *Fraülein* down the road," Wilhelm directed the child, refusing to look at Ruby. "At least as far as where the trail grows small."

"Yes, Papa," the boy cheerfully complied, taking Ruby's hand as he led her out the door.

She tried to meet Wilhelm's eyes once more, but his face was closed and tired, and he had turned away from her. Reluctantly she followed her tiny host out of the cabin.

They walked in silence for several moments. In the distance, Ruby could see that afternoon shadows were long beneath the Tree. Several wagons had already disappeared. Soon Wilhelm and Kelby would be alone with the mustard weed, miles and miles from anyone.

When they reached the place where the trail narrowed, Ruby turned to the child and asked, "Kelby, if your papa gets any worse, do you know how to go get help?"

Kelby nodded seriously. "Oh, yes, *Fraülein*. Do not worry. I am to put only the bridle on Hedda and climb on her bareback from the fence. I go on the trail that goes that way—" he pointed toward the east "—until the road bends. I go that way at the pile of rocks—" he pointed due north "—and soon I am at Mrs. Jasperson's."

Assuming he'd finished repeating his directions, Ruby was about to praise his good memory when he startled her by adding, "And then I tell her to take me to Reed's papa's ranch. If anything bad ever happens," he told her with firm conviction and assurance, "Papa promised that you would be the one to take care of me." When she stared at him incomprehensibly, he prodded her with halting words. "*Ja, Fraülein* Ruby?"

Honored and humbled, frightened and touched, Ruby could barely manage to speak. Somehow she managed to whisper her first fragmented German words to soothe the uneasy child. "*Ja, Kleines-Bärchen.* I would take care of you."

CHAPTER 10

IT WAS NOT YET AUTUMN when C.W. came back for Phoebe.

Reed spotted him first, but Ruby was the first to reach his side.

"C.W.! How nice of you to call." She knew that he thought her generous greeting was on her cousin's behalf, and to some extent it was. But even at a distance she had recognized Wilhelm's chestnut mare, Hedda. Even such a tenuous connection to the man was enough to send her scuttling down the steps to hear news of him. "Came in on the stage, did you?"

"Yes, indeed. I've only got a day and a half before it comes back through. I don't suppose your uncle's around at this hour of the day, is he?"

"My *uncle*?" Ruby echoed in disbelief. "Oh, C.W., you can't mean to say you're here on business!" Already she was starting to hurt for Phoebe.

But C.W. was grinning from ear to ear. "I think it would be more accurate to say that coming here is a pleasure, Ruby. But I do have business with your uncle, if you get my drift."

A small ache of jealousy coursed through Ruby's heart as she realized his intentions. Not because she had any designs on this impulsive, outgoing man whom her frivolous cousin so adored, but because she had never had a fine young man ride up to her father's house in the middle of a summer's afternoon and beg for her hand in marriage.

"As luck would have it, my uncle's down with a summer cold, C.W., so he decided to rest a bit this afternoon. But I'm sure that under the circumstances he could get out of bed long enough to hear you out."

Again he grinned, almost foolishly, as he wobbled off the horse. *Tenderfoot,* Ruby thought to herself. *Just like I was not so long ago.*

With that thought in mind, she called for Reed to walk and water Hedda. It would never do to be less than hospitable to one of Wilhelm's horses. He might forgive her for treating his wounds, but he'd never forgive her for leaving Hedda to heave and sweat in the sun.

"Kathleen, you go get your papa," she told the little girl who'd just bounded out of the kitchen announcing the visitor's presence at the top of her lungs. "And once I get you settled in the parlor, C.W., I do believe I'll mosey on down to the berry patch and tell my cousin that you're here."

He grinned helplessly. "I'd be much obliged if you'd do that, Miss Ruby. I'd surely be much obliged."

"He come back? He come back fer me?" Phoebe shrieked when she heard the news. "Yer not joshin' me, Ruby? Ya wouldn't do that ta me now, would ya?"

Phoebe's hands and apron were stained with berry

juice, but she paid no heed to her appearance as she galloped up to the house, crying and laughing all the way. Susanna, with all the wisdom of her not-quite-thirteen years, commented wryly, "I don't see why she's actin' like a chicken with its haid cut off. We all knew 'at sooner or later he'd be ridin' back this way."

The sober side of Ruby had to agree. By the time they got to the house, C.W. was shaking hands with Orville, but that was the end of his formal behavior. With a nod of approval from the other man, C.W. swept the nearly hysterical Phoebe into his arms and spun her around in the air half a dozen times, blubbering for all to hear that he'd wanted to wait for her to grow up some, for his business to flourish, for both of them to be sure. But he'd been unable to concentrate on anything in Los Angeles. He'd missed her so much it hurt . . . he was so afraid she'd find somebody else while he was gone . . . he couldn't live another day without her as his wife . . . His ingenuous litany went on and on.

Finally Ruby decided that she'd heard enough. Since nobody seemed to notice that she was standing on the porch, she decided to go down to the barn and talk to Hedda the way Wilhelm always did. Ruby rubbed the chestnut mare's ears and assured her that C.W. would be riding her back across the valley in the morning, so she'd only have to spend one night away from home. But sharing meaningless words with a tired old mare, even one as friendly as Hedda, did little to blot out the images in Ruby's mind.

She was sorely troubled by the scene she'd just witnessed, but she really wasn't sure why. She longed for the exhilarating sensation of romance that swirled between Phoebe and C.W., yet she would have been embarrassed by such a display from any man she knew. Surely there were quieter, more private means of showing one's affection! She tried to think of the traditional ways a man might declare his intentions—like bringing a lady flowers or breathing words like "sweetheart" or "darling" in her ear. But even this image failed to quell Ruby's unsettled feelings; with sudden, painful vision, she realized why.

Very soon the time might come when Joshua Casey would bring her flowers and call her "darling," his polished eloquence unbearably flattering to any sensible single woman in the valley. But from Joshua, the words were too smooth to have much meaning — too calculated to brush romantic longings across her listening ear.

It was a crusty string of Prussian syllables that Ruby longed to listen to, no matter what the words—a poignant rumble of guileless tenderness that would never be hers to hear.

The wedding trip to Los Angel bore no resemblance to Ruby's pathetic journey to Cayetano. For one thing, she and Phoebe didn't travel in a heavy old farm wagon with Uncle Orville. Joshua Casey took them in his finest carriage. They didn't stay in a remodeled adobe on straw tick mattresses, but at a glamorous mansion one night and a venerable old hacienda the next. Both families were "old and dear" friends of the Caseys. And visibly powerful and rich.

"I ain't never seen no house like this'un," Phoebe had gushed to the lady of the manor on the first night. "Even the Caseys' spread can't hold no candle to it."

Embarrassed both by Phoebe's grammar and her lack of guile, Ruby tacked on graciously, "We do appreciate your hospitality, ma'am. You're just as kind and thoughtful as I'd expect a friend of Joshua's to be."

The lady had smiled uncertainly, but later Ruby heard her whisper to Joshua, "It's hard to believe they're from the same family. Are you sure C.W. can teach that poor girl what she needs to know?"

The implications of that comment grew more clear to Ruby as they reached Los Angeles. In her native environment, Phoebe had just looked like Phoebe, and greenhorn C.W. had been the one who looked out of place. But in a thriving city of sixty thousand souls—its population having doubled since the onset of boosterism when the railroad had arrived a few years before—Phoebe looked like a country hayseed blown too far from topsoil to take root.

"Oh, Ruby, would ya jist look at it? A real city! Look at all th' people! Horses an' carriages ev'rywhere! Look at th' dresses! Look at that lady's palermine!" she gushed, vigorously pointing at a vivid blue cape. "Is that beaded silk, Ruby?"

Ruby could understand the girl's reaction; after all, she'd been just as shocked coming from Cincinnati to the Sycamore Valley. But after living there for six months, she was even more aware of the differences between modern life in a city—even one as small as Los Angeles—and day-to-day survival in the last outpost of the western frontier. The valley was only three days away from Los Angeles by stage or carriage, but it might as well have been on a distant island in the South Seas.

"Pa said I could buy a store-bought dress for th' weddin', Ruby! An' one fer ya too, since yer gonna be my bridesmaid 'n' all. Susanna's fit ta be tied that it ain't gonna be her, but she's too big to carry th' flowers an' too little ta stand beside me. Ma says her time'll come."

Ruby couldn't answer that; poor little Susanna

was likely to be wed in only three or four years' time. Maybe Ruby had waited too long to start the grand adventure of marriage, but deep in her heart she was sure that sixteen was too early for her cousin Phoebe.

The next month passed in a frenzy of activity. Ruby and Phoebe spent hours in dress stores, millinery shops, and parlors of influential ladies. They consulted with the preacher, the next-door neighbor, and several brides of recent months. They planned food and flowers and three days' lodging for the rest of the Caseys and the Barnetts "right down to a gnat's eyebrow," as Phoebe colorfully exclaimed.

Joshua took advantage of the time in Los Angeles to shower Ruby with all the cultural delights that she'd so sorely missed in the valley. He was busy during the day with various business dealings, but almost every night he and C.W. ushered the cousins to a concert, an opera, or a painting exhibition. They had dinner with countless "family friends," who were more than generous with their time and hospitality.

At first, Ruby found it very exciting to spend her time surrounded by fine music and splendid drama. It was stimulating to discuss these cultural joys with finely honed and articulate minds. She and Joshua spent hours discussing more plans for the church, a possible school, and Joshua's longterm dream of starting up a newspaper after the railroad came through the valley. He was certain that a major city would come right on the heels of the railroad, and he wanted to be a part of it. He wanted Ruby to be a part of it, too.

Six months ago she would have rejoiced at his future vision of Sycamore Valley, but now that she was once again ensconced in a city, she realized that life in California had changed her. As time went on, she grew weary of the noise and excitement of Los Angeles. She began to ache for something that no city had to offer.

For no reason at all, Ruby missed waking up to the sound of roosters. She noticed that the dirty street urchins, begging, reminded her of Kelby, and the freshly-scrubbed little boys in short pants and knickers seemed to look like him, too. All the city's fine foreign cuisine could not ease her longing for Aunt Clara's ranch-bred chicken 'n' dumplings.

She loved the rose gardens, but missed the mustard weed. She loved the stand of imported palms downtown, but thought them puny compared to the Tree. She loved the all-wool sack suits and golden watch chains of Joshua's business acquaintances, but she missed Uncle Orville's baggy trousers and dirty red suspenders.

Most of all, she missed Wilhelm.

She didn't really know it until the evening Joshua took her to see the *Merry Wives of Windsor*. The program was delightful, but the colorful posters in the lobby advertised a German comedy called *Otto*. It took no more than the sight of that one simple word in the Prussian tongue to strike a longing deep within her that no rational thought could deny.

She was quiet on the way home in the carriage. Joshua, for once sensitive to her feelings, waited until they were in seated in C.W.'s uncle's parlor before he began to talk. Even then, his words were slow and carefully chosen.

"Ruby, I know there are times when you'd—you'd rather be with somebody else but me."

Ashamed, Ruby couldn't think of a thing to say. Fortunately, he continued before she could speak.

"I can't make you any honest protestations of undying love, Ruby. I've never been love-cracked like

C.W. is. I'm not sure I'd want to be. But I think very highly of you—as highly as I've ever regarded any woman. I hope you know that by now."

Ruby couldn't bring herself to face him; she was still thinking about Wilhelm. It was an outrageously hot evening, and she found it hard to take a breath in her tight-laced corset—an unfamiliar torture after her summer on the ranch. Her jaunty feathered hat didn't set comfortably on her head like a slate cap; she longed to pull it off and let her hair down, just so she could breathe. She longed to smell the pungent aroma of chile plants that wafted up to her bedroom window from Phoebe's vegetable garden south of the barn. She longed for the sight of gentle blue eyes and an unkempt, bushy beard.

"I believe a man and woman should be well suited to each other, Ruby. Have the same interests, the same background, the same vision of the Lord as well as the same plans for their future on this earth."

It sounded terribly reasonable, but it wasn't really what Ruby wanted to hear from a man who was more than likely about to ask her to marry him. "And you think that's what it takes to make a good marriage?" she finally managed to say.

For a moment he studied her face—tired, troubled, hurt by his honesty. Then he admitted, "I'd like to think there's more to it than that, Ruby. My parents didn't have a thing in common but honest love, and I've never known a more devoted couple. My father—" he swallowed hard "—my father used to make up little jokes about my mother, jokes about San Francisco, just to hide the fact that he worshipped the ground she walked on. He was embarrassed by how obvious it was. And she—oh, I know it's hard to tell with that self-righteous mask she wears sometimes—but Ruby, she was devastated by my father's death."

Ruby met his eyes at last, touched by his searching honesty.

"It's been four years, but at night sometimes I still find her on the porch swing. Crying. She lets me sit there for a while and hold her in my arms. In the morning she always pretends it never happened."

It was the biggest piece of himself Joshua had ever offered Ruby, and his words had never warmed her more. It was as though a brick wall had crumbled between them; she didn't want to fight him anymore. "Joshua," she found herself admitting, "I like you so much better when you don't try to impress me." She graced him with an honest straight-from-the-heart smile.

To her surprise, Joshua looked genuinely touched and almost humble. "Do you realize, Miss Barnett, that this is the first time you've ever confessed to having any feeling for me at all?"

Ruby brushed away the cobwebs of guilt—the lingering sense that she was somehow betraying Wilhelm. What good did it do to love a man who had no interest in marriage? Joshua, on the other hand, showed every sign of wanting to deepen their relationship. He was entertaining, well-educated and well-bred. He was beginning to earn her affection, and to some extent, her respect.

She only hoped it would be enough.

It was at least a hundred degrees in the shade by Wilhelm's reckoning, and he was blistering in the sun. He should have been lying under the stand of live oaks where Kelby had fidgeted and whined for the last hour; instead, he was harnessed to a team of horses with a heavy iron plow bucking against his hands. The hard-packed clay fought him for every inch. It was strewn with rocks, and rattlers were so common this time of year that he always wrapped Val and Hedda's hoofs in burlap when they worked in the fields. He was still struggling to cultivate enough of the land to keep Kelby fed and clothed; he had a long way to go before he could try his hand at marketable oranges.

It was not an easy way to make a living, he'd concluded long ago. But then again, what was? At least here he was his own keeper. It was *his* land he was plowing, and only ambition kept him at his task. Nobody owned Wilhelm Morgen; nobody could tell him what to do.

Although some have surely tried, he thought grimly, recalling his recent encounter with the *Fraülein*. He'd only known one other woman with that kind of spirit—his grandmother on his father's side. A strong, sturdy woman, she was the only one of the family who had encouraged him to come to America. She hadn't understood his love of animals and growing things, but she'd realized that he would never feel complete until he ran his fingers through rich soil that covered *Morgen* land. She was the only member of the family who had not wept as the train had pulled out of sight that cloudy day in Frankfurt; yet she, among them all, was the one he still missed the most. He longed for Kelby to meet her just once before she died.

"Papa!" his son began to holler. "Papa, come here!"

Kelby was crying, which in itself was rare. The sound tore at Wilhelm; unconscious parental alarm coursed through his heart, eradicating his earlier irritation with his small son's petty complaints. A moment ago the boy had been crawling around on all fours like a puppy, howling and barking at a sleepy opossum hanging from one of the bumpy-skinned branches. Now his howl was of pain or fear.

"What is it, Kelby?" He abandoned the plow in an instant and rushed to the boy's side. "I am right here, *Kleines-Bärchen*."

Kelby held up one hand to show his father a deep puncture wound. For one terrible moment Wilhelm was sure that it had been made by a rattler's fangs. But he saw no sign of a serpent; on the ground lay a goat's head sticker the size of an acorn. From past experience Wilhelm knew how painful the stab of this spiny seed could be.

He sat down cross-legged under the trees and pulled the sobbing Kelby onto his lap. He cuddled his little one and whispered all the right things, yet somehow he felt as though he had let Kelby down. He'd brought him to a land without a church, without a school, without friends or family or even a pet dog! And for what? A futile, hopeless dream? *He's only a baby*, the *Fraülein* had told him. *You've let pride get the better part of love, and that little boy is the one who's going to pay the price.*

Wilhelm pushed away the troubling thoughts. Why did that woman upset him so? She had no right to come barging into his life. He'd told her, had he not, that he had no intention of getting to know her any better? No intention of marrying again?

He brushed off Kelby's hands and stood up. It didn't seem right for the horses to be standing in the sun while he rested in the shade. Yet he didn't really want to leave Kelby alone under the trees again. "Kelby, would you like to sit on Hedda while I finish the field? It is awfully hot out there, but—"

"*Ja*, Papa. I would like to go with you. I would like to wear the harness and help."

Wilhelm found a special smile for his son. "Someday you will do just that, small son. Someday you will help me work this land, and I will be very proud."

Kelby's little chest puffed out for just a moment. Then he said proudly, "But I help you now, do I not, Papa? When you were hurt, didn't I feed the chickens and the horses and try to milk the cow?"

He didn't want to think about his injury. The leg still bothered him; so did the *Fraülein's* silent, angry intrusion. The fact that she was right about so many things bothered him still more.

"Come along, then. Up on top you go."

He hoisted Kelby on to the gentle mare's back and forced the old harness lines over his own head. He clucked to Val and Hedda to start up again, then called a bit more forcefully when they were slow to move in the fading heat of early dusk.

Kelby kicked Hedda, then crawled over on Val's back to do the same. He had both horses moving freely before Wilhelm noticed the four dandies on horseback at the far edge of his freshly plowed field.

He was accustomed to the sight of a lone *vaquero* now and then, or even a pair of Indians. Every month or so a neighbor would pass by; only yesterday he'd seen Paul Hanson and his boy on their way back from Cayetano. Johnny had been kind enough to give Kelby a stick of peppermint candy.

But he knew in a glance that these men were outsiders. They did not belong in the valley. One had a bright red vest; another sported handguns in both holsters. All wore a look that made Joshua Casey seem downright humble.

Wilhelm knew they expected him to come to them, but he decided to finish plowing the field. Kelby was restless and the horses were tired. Whatever their business, it surely could wait another half hour.

They waited maybe ten minutes, until he finished

the furrow and turned the horses back around. Then they galloped toward him en masse, their sudden urgency alarming him in a way that made him wish he hadn't left his old Hawken in the barn.

"Papa," Kelby murmured as the foursome neared the plow, "I'm getting so hot, Papa. I need to drink some water. Can we go back to the house now?"

Wilhelm glared at the men and quickly shushed the boy. "This is not the time for whining, Kelby! Say nothing until I make them go."

He kept the horses moving, largely out of pride. He did not glance up until the one who looked like an undertaker pulled up a bit ahead of the others and began to speak. He recognized the voice at once; it was just as irritating as it had been the first time he'd met the speaker.

"Howdy-do, Mr. Morgen. You recall that Mr. Jenson and myself dropped by to chat with you not so long ago?"

Wilhelm glanced up indifferently. He remembered the two men from the railroad. But he said nothing.

"Still working hard, I see. Nobody to care for your boy?"

"Your business is with me," Wilhelm snapped. "A decent man would not trouble my small son."

The obese Mr. Jensen in the red vest gave Kelby an oily smile. Tobacco-stained teeth gave him a sinister look. "Little tyke looks plumb tuckered out, Mr. Morgen. Wouldn't we all be more comfortable up at the house?"

Livid, Wilhelm hollered out to the horses to press on. "You were not invited here. If you find no comfort, this is not my problem."

"So much for western hospitality," one of the other men said. His accent was strange to Wilhelm, as though he had not yet learned all the sounds of the language.

Kelby didn't seem to notice. In fact, Kelby didn't seem to appreciate the gravity of the situation at all, despite his huddled silence the last time these men came to call. "Papa," he whispered urgently, "I must have some water. If I could take Hedda up to the barn. Or I could run over to the river—"

"Hush, boy!" Wilhelm snapped, instinctively slipping into German. "Can't you see we are in grave trouble here?" Without looking at Kelby, who rarely needed to be scolded twice, he turned back to the four men and decided to end this charade. "If you come to ask about my land, my answer is the same. It will always be the same. Nothing you have to offer will ever mean more to me than the land I must make ready for my son." His eyes darkened as he studied each face, memorizing the men and horses that stood before him. "You are not welcome here. Do not come back again."

Proudly he turned back to his team, clucking them forward with a harsh tone that caused Val to lay back her ears. When Hedda did likewise, Wilhelm caught sight of a vision that made his heart go still as the air in the canyon when the desert wind sweeps the plains.

Kelby was slumped over the mare's neck, his tiny fingers clinging desperately to her shaggy black mane while his feet sprawled limply across her withers. His cherub's eyes were closed and his bright red face was flushed with a kind of fever that had nothing to do with the heat of the sun.

"And Ruth said, Entreat me not to leave thee, or to return from following after thee: for whither thou goest, I will go; and where thou lodgest, I will lodge: thy people shall be my people, and thy God, my God. . . ."

Ruby read the sacred words again and again, but

she could not focus on their meaning. She blamed the stuffy heat that permeated the upstairs bedroom; she even blamed the emptiness of the four-poster that Phoebe had once graced with her childish laughter and woman's dreams.

This was Ruby's first night back at Uncle Orville's ranch. Almost four days had passed since she'd walked down the aisle on Joshua Casey's arm as a bridesmaid. Almost four days since she'd realized, with pathetic, inescapable clarity, that she didn't really want to be Joshua Casey's wife.

She couldn't explain it, even to herself. She didn't want to grow old alone. She ached for children, for a home, for a man whose ideas enriched her own. The last thing she wanted was a man who was too stubborn for his own good—who would rather kill a grizzly for her in secret than show up at her door in broad daylight with a handful of flowers! But she couldn't marry Joshua Casey when Wilhelm Morgen still lived in her heart.

She laid the Bible down on the bed and gave up the pretense of reading. Restlessly she tugged on her coral calico dress again and crept downstairs. No one was up and about. It was already after midnight, but it was so hot outside even at this hour that she didn't need a shawl. And now that the bear was dead, there was nothing to fear in the solitary midnight walk.

"I miss you, Papa," she whispered to the night sky as she strolled past the barn. "You would have told me what to do."

She whisked away the hint of a tear and forced herself to be practical. Phoebe's marriage, so sudden when she was so young, had made Ruby's single state even more noticeable than it had been before. She was running out of time; she was running out of choices. If Joshua were interested, he would be a good husband. They had so much in common! Leading the prayer meeting together had been so satisfying for both of them, a hint of the kind of partnership they might develop in the years to come. Joshua's home needed a mistress with some eastern polish. If he were right about the effect of the railroad on Sycamore Valley, his future business dealings would require it.

So why do I look to the north . . . to a one room adobe hut with an immigrant pioneer who's told me straight out that he doesn't want me for his wife?

"Because he told his son to come to me in time of trouble," she admitted to herself. "He would trust me with the one person he holds dear to him in this world."

But it was the other person he still held dear—no longer of this world but of the next—who kept him away from Ruby. She tried to resent Oma Morgen, but she could not find such meanness in her soul. She had only pity for this devoted woman who had loved Wilhelm enough to give her own life as penance for his dreams.

She returned to the house an hour later, with none of her thoughts resolved. To her surprise there was a lamp burning in the parlor when she opened the door.

"Ruby?" a tense voice reached her from behind her uncle's desk. "Where have you been?"

She poked her head around the corner and met Orville's grave blue eyes. "I couldn't sleep. I went for a walk."

His expression lightened. "Did it help?"

Ruby was puzzled. "What do you mean, Uncle Orville?"

"I don't mean to pry, Ruby, but you've been acting so . . . out of sorts since Phoebe's wedding that I've been wondering just where your thoughts have been taking you." He walked over to her side and laid one hand on her shoulder, the touch as gentle as a baby's breath. "I wish I could do more to make you happy," he admitted softly. "I feel as though your father entrusted you to me. It's so much greater a responsibility than if . . . he were just away on business somewhere."

His words were so wistful that Ruby realized, "You miss him, too, Uncle Orville? For twenty years you've lived without him—"

"And for twenty years before that, I spent every day by his side." He shook his head. "I always knew I could go back, Ruby. I always thought that sooner or later, he'd come to see me or I'd go back to see him. But now he's gone like my brother Henry. It just isn't the same."

Ruby blinked a few times and looked away. "No, it's not the same."

Orville gave her a moment's privacy before he asked, "Do you want to tell me what happened between you and Joshua in Los Angeles? I admit I'm a bit perplexed. I've known that boy since he was knee-high to a grasshopper, and even though he can be a bit high and mighty at times, I know he'd never set out to hurt any woman, especially one of my kin. If he—"

Ruby cut him off. "He didn't do anything, Uncle. He's always been quite nice to me." She tried to find words to explain what had happened, but all she could picture was the sight of Phoebe's glowing face as she promised her life to C.W. Warren. Ruby, gussied up to beat the band in her blue taffeta bridesmaid gown, had wondered if she'd ever look at Joshua and feel so delirious when the preacher pronounced them man and wife. Then she'd taken Joshua's right arm as they'd left the church together, and suddenly she'd thought of Wilhelm's bloody shoulder and wondered if it had healed—

"It's just that . . . when I look at Joshua, I—"

She never got to finish the story. The rumble of hoofbeats in the lane arrested her uncle's attention.

"One horse. Running hard," Uncle Orville declared, his ear cocked toward the door. He glanced at the clock on his desk which he wound so meticulously every night and shook his head. "Go upstairs and stay out of sight 'til I call you, gal."

"Uncle Orville?" she asked, panic filling her heart. "Who do you think it is?"

He shook his head and hurried toward the door. "Doesn't matter who. Any way you look at it, it's got to be bad news."

CHAPTER 11

IT WAS WILHELM. She knew it in her heart even before she saw his beloved form slide off the gasping black mare. A blur of images constricted her heart. *How unlike him to ride a horse into the ground. He's hollering—he's begging for help! I've never seen him go anywhere without Kelby.*

It was the last thought, tucked in so brutally among the others, that caused Ruby to ignore her uncle's orders and rush to the door.

"Wilhelm, what's happened? What's wrong with Kelby?"

For a moment neither one of them noticed Orville, the voice of reason trying to make sense of the midnight summons. But Orville, no doubt, assumed that Wilhelm had come to *him* for help. He did not yet realize that he'd covered half a day's ride in two hours just to speak to Ruby.

"Cholera," he breathed raggedly. "Just like Mo Jasperson. Just like all the others. You must save my baby bear, *Fraülein*. You are the only one who can."

Ruby stood rigidly in the doorway, realizing what he was asking. He had not come to her for comfort, for support in his time of crisis. He had not even asked her to help him clean his house or do his chores or entertain his child. He had asked for a miracle; he had asked her to save his son. From a deadly disease for which there was no cure.

She could not speak to Wilhelm; she could not sever the last rawhide strand of his lariat of hope. Instead she turned to Orville and commanded in a voice that was firm and calm, "Saddle up two horses, Uncle. The best you've got. I'll go get Hank to help you."

Ruby knew that her city-park riding skills were about to be put to the severest kind of test, but she didn't give a moment's thought to the impropriety of riding astride. She lifted her eyes to Wilhelm's, her widow's peak framing her lovely features like a halo honoring an angel. Her determination offered him strength.

She lay a tender hand on his anguished face and promised, "If there's any way this side of Heaven that I can save your son, you know I'll do it, Wilhelm. And the very first thing I'm going to do is—*pray*."

And pray they did, for five long days and endless nights. But there was no change in Kelby.

Wilhelm had left him at Sarah Jasperson's, where the disease had already taken its toll and passed by those who were still alive. He'd been torn between taking the boy directly to the *Fraülein* and sparing him such a long trip in the wagon when he was so weak. Eventually he'd ridden to the Barnett ranch alone, terrified that his son would die before he got back.

The *Fraülein* had not offered a single complaint

during the galloping ride to the Jaspersons. Nor had she succumbed to weariness or fear or the leaden hopelessness that had taken over Wilhelm's body and soul. With infinite patience she sat by little Kelby, keeping him cool, forcing him to drink, propping him up when he coughed and choked—praying for him when he was still.

And when she was not at Kelby's bedside, it was Wilhelm himself whom she tended. With quiet determination she made him eat and soothed him into restless sleep with his head on the kitchen table. Somehow she made him talk about his citrus dreams and his family in the old country. Once she even got him to share the tale of his terrible guilt and loneliness that first dark year in America.

And through it all—through the dark days and even darker nights full of unanswered questions about fate and the future and God's unerring will—came a slow sense of discovery that gradually permeated Wilhelm's grief-laden heart. *She was right to be angry with the way I have lived my life here,* he realized. *My pride has been greater than my love for my son.* If he'd had any doubts about the matter, these last few days had brought reality into excruciatingly sharp focus. Kelby needed friends and neighbors and the security that one man alone in the wilderness could never give him. He needed a mother so desperately! And if he lived through this terrible ordeal, his right to that maternal devotion outweighed his father's need to nurse his lingering grief for the woman who had died giving birth to the boy amidst the tossing seas.

It was obvious, even to the most proud and stubborn of men, whom Kelby's new mother was meant to be.

The fever broke on the morning of the sixth day.

It was not yet dawn and Sarah was still in bed. Wilhelm had spent the last hour prowling between the house and the barn, too restless to sleep—too fatigued to stay by Kelby's side.

Ruby herself was too exhausted to think at all; it took her a moment to realize that something in the room had changed. The sunny smile on Kelby's face seemed unreal until he spoke. "*Fraülein* Ruby, what are you doing here?"

Choking back her joy, Ruby reached down to hug her tiny charge. Weakly he clutched her neck. She was too relieved to speak, too moved to hide her tears. Yet she didn't want to frighten Kelby. Now was not the time to tell him how close he'd come to death.

"I came over to visit while you were sick," Ruby informed him with forced nonchalance. "When you feel a little better, I will make you something to eat."

"Cookies like Reed's mama makes?" he asked, blue eyes mischievous for just a second.

Ruby smiled. "When you are well enough."

"I don't know if Papa will allow it."

Ruby was glad he remembered his father's rules; at the moment he didn't even realize that he was not in his father's house. "Would you like to see your papa?" she asked him.

Kelby nodded. "If he can spare the time, *Fraülein*. He works so very hard."

Ruby squeezed the boy's shoulder and moved quickly to the door. She found Wilhelm sitting on the Jasperson's porch, leaning against a wooden pillar. "Wilhelm," she called out, shaking him urgently. "He's awake. He's talking. His fever has broken!"

Wilhelm's eyes flashed open. He bolted to his feet. "Again say this to me, *Fraülein*?" he begged her.

"He's going to be all right!"

Without thinking, Wilhelm threw both arms around Ruby and buried his face in her neck. His rough beard scratched her delicate skin; his relief was so physical that she could feel his heart beating in time with her own. Fiercely she hugged him back, equally delirious with Kelby's recovery, before she questioned the propriety of the embrace.

But she did not step back, and Wilhelm did not try to release her. For once he made no effort to hide his feelings. He pulled her closer yet, crushing her shoulders against his massive chest as he rocked her slowly in anguished relief.

"*Fraülein*," he whispered, his breath warming her face, "Tell me again. Tell me my son will live."

Ruby hugged him as hard as she could; without thinking she pressed a loving kiss on his cheek. "He's going to live, Wilhelm. He's going to be all right."

Slowly Wilhelm put her from him, but he kept a steady grip on her shoulders. "You are sure, *Fraülein*? My son will live? The Lord will not take him from me this time?"

Ruby reached up to touch his roughened face with both hands. She was shaking with joy and fatigue. "He's going to be fine, Wilhelm. It will take a while—he is very weak—but he's not going to die."

For a moment Wilhelm closed his eyes. A tiny shudder passed through his body. Then he released Ruby and straightened.

"I will go to see my son. And then, . . . when he is asleep again . . . you will kneel down with me and give thanks, will you not?"

Ruby met his intense gaze with tenderness and renewed strength. "*Ja*, Wilhelm. We will give thanks."

Ruby stayed at Sarah Jasperson's for two more days before Wilhelm brought her home. They decided to ride over to the Barnetts' ranch together so he could trade his borrowed horse for Val.

"This is really quite a pretty ride," Ruby commented as the horses picked their way over the well-marked road. Now that it was daylight and everything was calm, she was embarrassed to be seen riding astride with her rumpled skirt hanging down both sides of the horse. "Quite a change from our last trip together."

Wilhelm gave her one of his rare and radiant smiles. It was such a joy to see him happy. "Many things have changed for us, *Fraülein*," he assured her. "You have indeed brought the miracle."

"The Lord brought the miracle, Wilhelm. I just helped out a little bit."

He was silent for a moment. Ruby turned back to the road that lay ahead, enjoying the sight of tiny green and yellow birds chirping from the top of a stalk of milkweed. It was still so hot and dry that most of the valley was brown, but even under these conditions there was beauty to be found on such a day.

"Mrs. Jasperson was very good to help us," Wilhelm declared as though there had been no break in the conversation. "She did much of what you did, but it was not the same, *Fraülein*."

Ruby looked at him quizzically. "I'm not sure I know what you mean."

He thought for a minute, struggling with the English words. "Mrs. Jasperson cares for Kelby. She thinks he is a good boy and she thinks I am a hard worker."

Ruby grinned. "She's right on both counts."

He shook his head. "You know—you know the parts of me that no one else can see. You care enough to get angry with me and share the tears in my heart."

A strange sensation waved through her body at the serious intent of his words. Wilhelm had never talked to her like this, and although they were riding along on horseback with the morning sun already drying their skin, there was something in his words that made her think of moonlight.

Yet his next words took her by surprise. "It is because of Kelby. He is not just a small child to you. He is not even dear to you like your little cousin Reed. Kelby is—it is as though he were your own son."

Ruby could not deny the words, nor could she explain them. She didn't know if she loved little Kelby only for himself or because he was a part of Wilhelm. All she knew was that while he'd lain ill, a part of her had been dying. Now that he would live, she was whole again. Oma Morgen, Ruby was certain, had loved the child no more than she.

"*Fraülein*, you should be his mother now, should you not?"

Ruby glanced up at him, startled. "If I ever have a son, Wilhelm, I'd be proud for him to be just like Kelby."

It was not the answer he seemed to be looking for. "You do not understand. I want for you to be his mother."

Her heart began a strange, dizzy waltz across the huge vacuum of her ribcage. Her eyes began to blur and her tongue grew thick and dry. *I'm exhausted,* she reminded herself. *I'm too weary to make sense of his words.*

"He told me that if anything ever happened to you, I was the one you wanted to raise him, Wilhelm. I promised him that I would, and I make the same promise to you—no matter what my . . .

situation might be."

He raised his hands in exasperation and turned sharply in the saddle to face her. "*Fraülein*, it is not like you to be so slow to understand! I want you to be his mother *now*. I want you to cook good food and set it on the table for him. I want you to sew his clothes and care for him when he is sick. I want you to hold him on your lap and tell him stories!"

"I do that when I can, Wilhelm," she told him tersely, marveling at his single-minded denseness. "But all propriety aside, I live too far away—"

"You need to live with us!" he exploded, more emotion in his voice than Ruby had ever heard before. "You need to set down roots on Morgen land. You need—" he paused and wrung out the words with excruciating care "—you need to be my wife."

Ruby's horse stopped of his own volition; she didn't have to touch the reins. Wilhelm's face seemed to slide into pieces and then merge back together again. Wonder and joy and disbelief battled in her heart. For several moments she stared at him, trying to focus on his beloved face. He didn't say a word.

"You are . . . you are asking me to *marry* you, Wilhelm?" she choked out incredulously.

"Did I not say as much?" His tone was terse.

Ruby took a deep breath. "You told me . . . not so very long ago . . . that you would never marry again."

"And you told me, not so long ago, that I had been very selfish to deprive my son of the people he needs. I am not a stupid man, *Fraülein*. I have learned much about God's will in the last few terrible days."

She studied his eyes and tried to read the welter of feelings there. Determination, yes. Embarrassment. Concern for his beloved child. A request for marriage that surely came on the heels of his great relief that Kelby's life had been spared and gratitude for Ruby's own small part in his recovery. It was nice—it was marvelous—to conceive of a lifetime as Wilhelm's wife, a lifetime as little Kelby's mother. But something was missing in this unorthodox proposal. Memories of C.W.'s trip to Uncle Orville swam through her mind. Not the formality of his request for Phoebe's hand, but the magical tenderness Ruby had seen so many times in his eyes. A majestic adoration that by no fantasy of her heart's longing could she read now on Wilhelm's tense and weary face.

"Wilhelm, before I give you an answer, there is something I need to understand," she said as evenly as her chest-pounding pulse would allow. "You are asking me to marry you so that . . . I can be Kelby's mother?"

"Of course!" he proclaimed with relief that she finally understood him. "What better reason could there be?"

Long after dinner had been served, Ruby heard Aunt Clara come in and set a tray of food on the bureau dresser. She had pleaded exhaustion and fled to her room the moment she and Wilhelm had arrived, and her aunt had mercifully asked no questions. Wilhelm was always silent, and under the circumstances nobody expected him to be very chatty. He'd asked Orville how Val was doing and thanked him for sending Hank to take over the chores in his absence, but he made no further comments to Ruby in front of the others. He'd already said everything there was to say on the trail.

"Thank you, Aunt Clara," Ruby said softly from the bed. "I'm really not hungry now, but maybe later I'll be up to something."

She wasn't sure why she spoke up; she could have let Aunt Clara disappear without a word. Subconciously maybe she'd mulled things over alone long enough. She desperately needed the comfort of another woman who knew what it was like to love a quiet, pragmatic man. In some ways, Wilhelm was a lot like Uncle Orville.

"Ya ain't took sick now, Ruby, have ya?" Aunt Clara asked with mock sternness, crossing the room to touch Ruby's brow. "Ya look a mite peaked."

Ruby shook her head. "No. I just . . . it's been a while since I've had a good night's sleep."

Aunt Clara stood there, looking down at the bed, her huge bulk a welcome shadow against the fading afternoon light. "I don't think it's yer body what's all wore out, gal. Maybe there's somethin' not right in yer heart."

Ruby shifted uncomfortably in the bed. Privacy was all she wanted now, wasn't it? Her aunt had never understood Wilhelm. How could she now? Besides, Ruby didn't know if it was advice or comfort she needed most. Or just some kind of miracle.

When Ruby didn't answer, Aunt Clara hesitated, then sat down on the edge of the bed. "Ruby, I know we're not cut outta th' same piece a cloth. Ya talk so purty an' I know ya think I'm jist a simple hayseed. But I *am* a woman, gal, an' I know a woman's heart." She took Ruby's hand. "It's love that's makin' ya feel sa bad, hon. Couldn't be nothin' else. I've had th' same sickness more than once myself."

Ruby had never expected to find herself sharing secrets with her aunt; yet so many things had changed. After a moment's tense silence, she blurted out, "Oh Aunt Clara, what do you do when you love a man so much it hurts, but he asks you to marry him for all the wrong reasons?"

The older woman sighed. "Depends on th' reasons. If he's jist usin' ya ta make a point ta somebody else—"

"No, it's nothing like that. He just wants a . . . a housekeeper, a nurse, a mother to his son. It's almost as though Kelby asked for a mama for Christmas, so Wilhelm's going to try to find him one."

Aunt Clara didn't bat an eye when Ruby revealed the name of the man she loved. "Wilhelm Morgen is the stubbornest man alive, Ruby. Ain't no way even Kelby could talk him inta somethin' he didn't wanna do."

Ruby sighed. "Oh, he's *willing* to marry me, Aunt Clara, but he doesn't really *want* to. At least . . . not for any of the reasons that C.W. wanted to marry Phoebe."

"Pshaw, gal! Don't ya know any better'n that?" Clara shook her head. "Phoebe only knows 'bout one kinda love; she ain't old enough ta know there's others. She's right fond a C.W., but she don't love him now like she's gonna when she's old. Married love is like a hearty stew . . . th' longer it simmers on th' stove the tastier it gits." She paused to let her words sink in. "Now ya ain't been married yet, Ruby, but ya ain't no young'un, neither. Yer old enough ta know that what a man *says* an' what a man *feels* ain't always th' same thing. Especially a man like Wilhelm Morgen. I imagine he's got his own ways a showin' love."

And what are his ways? Ruby asked herself. *He's shown me his love for Kelby. But does he have any love for me?*

"Like me'n Orville, gal. When we was first courtin' I wanted him ta fuss all over me an' when he wouldn't say he loved me, I got mad an' give him th' gate. Then he went ta California an' I purt near cried my eyes out fer three months. That winter I started seein' this other fella. Talkin'est man I ever knew! When he asked me ta marry him, I ast my ma what ta do. I was hopin' fer a miracle."

She seemed to grow a little prettier as she spoke. "Well, my ma, she knowed what was in my heart, sa she done wrote ta Orville an' tol' him his time was 'bout up. First thing ya knowed, he shows up on th' porch, skinny as a rail, wearin' a coat what wouldna kept a flea warm. He didn't say nothin' 'bout lovin' me then, neither. He jist said he'd come back fer his bride, an' he weren't gonna ask again." She smiled at the memory. "We was hitched th' next day."

Dusk was waiting outside the window by the time Clara finished her story. Ruby didn't know what to say . . . to her aunt or to Wilhelm.

"What did ya tell him, hon?" Clara finally asked her.

Ruby sighed. "I told him I'd need to think about it. He looked like I'd slapped him in the face."

"Then like as not, he won't as' again, gal. If ya want him, you'll have ta bring th' subject up next time ya see him."

Ruby sat up and fought the urge to weep. "How do I do that, Aunt Clara? Do I say, 'Oh, by the way, Wilhelm, I've thought it over and I'd like to marry you, after all?' Or do I ask him outright, 'Can't you say something to convince me that you might be a little tiny bit in love with me, too?' Or do I just swallow my pride altogether and ride over there tomorrow to see how Kelby is? Or just admit I'm there to see Wilhelm? It could be months before I run into him again!"

Suddenly Aunt Clara's arms were around her as the tears of confusion and exhaustion broke forth. Slowly the big woman rocked her niece as she struggled with her heart.

"I can't answer that, Ruby. A woman ain't got no business crawlin' fer a man, but then again pride never kept nobody company in her old age, neither. All I can tell ya is—" she pulled back to wipe Ruby's tear-streaked face with her pudgy, loving fingers "—whatever ya tell him next time ya meet is what yer gonna have ta live with all th' rest a yer born days."

He knew he had made a mistake.

Kelby was home, asleep in his bed, and the animals were still in good shape after four days in Hank Barnett's care. But Wilhelm was coming unraveled.

It was inconceivable that the *Fraülein* did not know how much she meant to him—enough to swallow his stiff-necked pride and admit that Morgen land was no longer complete without her sterling presence. She knew everything else about him, even things that he himself did not yet know. How could she be too blind to realize that by asking her to be Kelby's mother, he had given her the highest honor he could bestow on any woman? Why must he shower her with words of lesser kinds of love when he had already proven that he prized her above all others?

"*Frauen!*" he lamented, absently picking up a piece of manzanita from the pile he kept for a fire. He always whittled when he was nervous. It helped him get his thoughts in order. Tonight he was not the only one who was uneasy; Val kept fretting, pawing at the pasture gate. He'd already gone down there once to check on her.

A new thought struck Wilhelm as he carved. It was possible, was it not, that the *Fraülein* had understood his feelings very well, but had deliberately feigned misunderstanding to avoid refusing him outright? He was not the only man courting this woman!

Courting?! He choked on the word. He had never courted a woman. He did not know how. He had known Oma since childhood, and their marriage had been assumed long before either of them had given it any thought. He had always loved her as a friend, and only after she had become his wife had he grown to love her as a woman. How quickly that brief time had been snatched away!

He made a deep cut in the chunk of wood and asked himself what he had to offer the *Fraülein*. She came from a world of culture and education that was foreign to him. On the trail today she had said, "I'll have to think about it, Wilhelm. I need to marry a man who can fill my life with music."

"It is Joshua Casey who can give you music," he'd retorted, deliberately misunderstanding her metaphor. "Somehow he might find a way to buy you a piano and deliver it in the wilderness. Even if I had the money, I would never toss it away so carelessly when there are seedlings to plant and land to plow and hogs that would grow fat with better grain."

The realization that Joshua could give Ruby things that he could not always incensed him. Never more than now. Had Joshua already asked her to marry him? Was she deciding between the two? If so, he didn't stand a chance. No woman who could be happy married to a man who rode a lame horse would ever choose to marry Wilhelm Morgen.

He was still gnawing on the last thought when he heard Val's cry of alarm join Hedda's shrill neigh from just south of the barn. Suddenly the cow was mooing. The noise from the chicken coop could have meant a lynx or a coyote, but the larger animals would only react to a big cat or a bear.

Wilhelm grabbed his Hawken and cast a final glance at his sleeping son before he latched the door. Stealthily he headed toward the barn.

He was only halfway there when the dark scent flailed in his nostrils, and his eyes rose in panic to the sight in the east. There was no moon and the sky should have been black as tar, but it looked like a wood stove thick with leaping flames on a freezing winter's eve.

With dark, speechless terror he realized that the valley was on fire.

CHAPTER 12

FOR THE SECOND TIME IN A FORTNIGHT, the Barnett family was awakened to the sound of hoofbeats in front of the house. This time it was a wagon with two horses and a cow tied to the end. A baby screamed its terror and two toddlers clung mutely to their mother's skirts.

"Fire!" Paul Hanson hollered as his team pulled into the yard. "Fire, Orville! Brush fire headin' this way!"

Ruby ran to the window and looked to the east. The angry red sky mocked the fire that still raged in her heart. She bolted into the next room to still the pounding hearts of Susanna and Kathleen, who met her wide-eyed and sleepy at the door.

She could hear Hank barking orders at Reed. Orville roared out of his room wearing only a pair of trousers, while Clara followed him in her nightdress.

"Orville! Clara! D'ya hear me?" Paul called up again, banging on the door. "Fire all over th' valley!"

They all met outside at the same time. Kathleen

began to whine, but Ruby shushed her in an instant. She wished she could do the same for her own heart.

"If'n it stays on its path, it might pass ya by, Orville. But there's no way a knowin' what th' wind'll do."

"I know," her uncle decided quickly. "We can't afford to take any chances." He glanced at Clara for just an instant. "All of you get in the wagon. Hank and I'll bring the horses. There's no time for anything else."

Nobody had to tell Clara twice. Paul Hanson plopped her on the wagon bed like a sack of potatoes while Orville tossed up Reed and both girls. But when he reached for Ruby, she met his eyes with a new brand of terror.

"It's heading straight for the Tree, Uncle. No neighbors will go that way to warn him. He hasn't really slept for days because of Kelby, and he won't be as alert as he normally would be. If—"

Orville shook his head impatiently, hoisting Ruby up against her will. "It takes half a day to get to Wilhelm's, Ruby. The fire will be there in less than an hour."

She tugged on his arm in desperation. "But Uncle Orville, I rode to Sarah's in two hours. There's a back way and—"

"And only Wilhelm knows the way and besides, Ruby, *we would still get there too late*." He paused for just a second to treat the desperation in her eyes. He laid one hand on her face. "There is nothing any of us can do to save his ranch, Ruby. If he makes it out alive, he'll have enough on his plate without having to bear your death or mine or Hank's! He'll need us all to recover from the blow."

She covered her face with her hands as the wagon started to roll. In the rumble of the wheels she heard her uncle's last words repeated like a mournful litany: "I'm sorry, hon. I'm sorry, hon. I'm sorry, hon. . . ."

And above the thunder in her heart, the baby continued to cry.

There was only one southern route out of the valley—an old Chumash foot-path over Manzanita Mountain. The Hansons' buckboard couldn't handle the steep grade of the narrow trail, and eventually the ragtag caravan stopped halfway up the slope and gathered to peer across the bone-dry bed of horse-high mustard weed that they had all called home.

"It's headin' due west," Hank concluded, still perched atop his favorite bay. "It'll go clear to th' coast an' burn itself out, Pa."

Orville nodded. "Looks like we're safe up here. But I can't tell about my ranch. If the fire passes it by, it'll be by a gnat's eyebrow."

Paul Hanson said nothing. They all knew that he would find nothing left on his land at all.

It was not yet dawn when half a dozen other horses and a mule dragged themselves up the hill, carrying what was left of the Carlson family. By then despair was joining the panic which gripped the three families that tearfully welcomed each other on the shoddy trail up Manzanita Mountain. One unspoken question haunted them all. *Are we the only survivors?*

It was Aunt Clara who first decided, "We outta pray fer th' others. We need ta thank th' good Lord that our own kin is safe."

And so they prayed—men, women and children—though not one of them had thought to bring a Bible. They knelt in the dirt and breathed in the acrid, smoky air, holding hands as though they were of one body and one blood. And there on the hilltop, far away from the revival tent and Joshua

Casey's best going-to-meeting suit and Ruby's favorite songbook, the first church of Sycamore Valley was truly born.

Four hours later they stood there, watching the fire consume the land they had called home. It was a vibrant blaze that seemed to devour everything for miles. In the dark it had been difficult to tell just how far it had spread; the south side of the *Rancho* still looked more brown than black. The only thing Ruby was sure of was that flames had enveloped the ranch at the base of the Tree.

She did her part to soothe the children. She offered up her most heartfelt prayers. But her eyes never left the first turn of the trail, never stopped seeking the tattered form of a tall, tired man and a precious, smiling child.

It was a vigil that went on all day and all the next night, long after Orville and Hank had ridden back down the hill to see what was left of the ranch. The family praised God when they learned that all the buildings were still intact, and the Carlsons and the Hansons rejoiced right along with them. Without discussion, they all knew that the Barnett ranch would be their home for as long as they needed a place to stay.

Ruby and Clara brought out food and blankets as the guest list kept on growing. The McConnells, the Watsons and the O'Rileys arrived, battered and footsore. The Lissens and the Kentons straggled in from the east, but Sarah Jasperson was the only arrival from the northern end of the valley.

"Th' fire chased me all th' way to th' rock pile by th' road," she confessed. "Surely th' good Lord had his arm 'round my shoulder, or I never would've gotten th' young'uns this far."

Ruby faced her for just a minute, asking her

wordless question with tearful brown eyes. The two women embraced eacher other in anguished silence as Sarah whispered, "There's always hope, hon."

They broke apart as two horses, white with lather, galloped up the main road; Ruby all but ceased to breathe as she waited for the riders to reach the house. Fresh hope flooded her senses.

"It's Joshua Casey!" Kathleen shouted a moment later. "An' Joe-David, too!"

Everybody cheered—except for Ruby. She was relieved to see both brothers safe and sound, but she had never worried about them greatly. Everybody knew that their house was the farthest south of any ranch in the valley. The folks from the northern side were the ones who would have been devastated by the fire—the folks least likely to have made it out in time.

Ruby couldn't bring herself to greet the newcomers. Abruptly she burst into tears and ran to the barn. She knelt in the straw and began to pray. She couldn't believe that God had taken Kelby and his father from her; she couldn't believe she hadn't rejoiced and promised to be Wilhelm's wife the first instant he'd asked.

Yet she knew that too much time had elapsed since the fire to expect many more survivors. If Wilhelm had gotten out alive, he would surely have arrived by now—unless he'd been too proud to come at all. Surely not! Not even Wilhelm would have left the valley without assuring her that he was alive!

"Ruby?" an urgent voice interrupted her thoughts. "Dear God in Heaven, are you all right?"

She glanced up to greet Joshua, but she could not feign great joy at the sight of him. "I am not hurt, Joshua," she admitted, her tone weak and hopeless.

"But there is not a single one among us who is truly *all right*."

Joshua did not look well either. His face was pasty-white; for once, even his clothes were rumpled and stained with sweat. "I can't begin to tell you how worried I've been," he confessed, helping Ruby to her feet. "I never realized . . . I really never knew . . ." He stopped abruptly when he saw her blank stare. He seemed to know she could not hear him.

The truth was, Ruby was in mourning for the man she had already chosen to be her husband. She could not bear to share her grief with someone who had not shared her love for Wilhelm. She was in no condition to appreciate the tender confession of undying love from some other man.

"Excuse me, Joshua," she told him distantly. "I think I'm needed in the house."

A hurt look settled on his face as she left him there. Later she might regret giving him pain, but at the moment Ruby did not have enough room in her heart to grieve for a wealthy man who had lost nothing in the fire. Mutely she passed the others who gathered on the porch and in the yard, sharing food and words of comfort as they tried to plan their futures.

Ruby could not fight the flow of tears as she dragged herself up the stairs. Nor could she accept the fact that she would never see Wilhelm or Kelby again.

Her moment of privacy was short-lived. She had not yet closed her own door when Aunt Clara's shrill voice reached her from Kathleen and Susanna's room.

"Ruby! Come here right quick!"

Ruby responded to the summons with less than radiance. But when she found her aunt staring out the window, pointing to what appeared to be no more than a stick figure in the distance, she began to shake all over.

"Looky this poor feller, Ruby! He's so tired he can hardly put one foot in front a th' other. Could that be Wilhelm comin'?"

Ruby pressed her face to the glass, her heart clattering with wild new hope as she strained her eyes to see the vaguest of upright forms in the twilight. *Dear God, forgive my lack of faith! Dear God, if there is any way at all. . . .*

"Ruby . . ." her aunt repeated in a voice stripped of her earlier joy, "if that's brother Wilhelm, why is he leadin' a riderless horse?" She stared for a moment before she added in a low, dark tone, "Ruby, I don't see no sign a Kelby. No sign a th' boy atall."

Fatigue blurred the lines of the ranch house before him; for a moment he thought it was a mirage. He'd had nothing to eat or drink for twenty-four hours while he'd galloped on horseback, taken a back-wrenching fall, and walked twenty-miles with the dead weight of a sleeping child on his shoulders. Only some internal clock kept him moving forward. *Got to get Kelby to the* Fraülein, his benumbed spirit called out. *Can't collapse on the prairie. Can't ride a lame horse. Got to get Kelby to safety.*

He almost ran into the man on the horse. No, there were two men . . . two horses. Casey's horses. Yes, he knew the gray mare. There were words of welcome . . . genuine joy . . . from Joe-David. Surely he was dreaming now. It was Joshua who dismounted, pulled Kelby gently off his back and handed him to his brother. Joshua, who half-lifted Wilhelm into the saddle, his hands firm but kind. Joshua, who followed on foot, leading poor old hobbling Hedda.

Wilhelm was long past speech, but somehow he made it clear that Kelby had to ride with him. Reluctantly Joe-David returned the boy whom Wilhelm cradled in his arms. He took Wilhelm's reins and led the other horse. Wilhelm never noticed.

There were faces everywhere in the barnyard. Faces full of tears, yet somehow full of joy as they welcomed him. Women who hugged him and small children who tugged at his legs; men who clapped him on the back as he wearily slid off the horse. Martha Hanson was praising God and Sarah Jasperson was reaching for little Kelby. Even noisy Clara Barnett's voice was a balm to his beleaguered spirit.

But still he did not yield to his exhaustion; still he tightly gripped his boy in his arms. There was one face he had yet to find, and the possibility that she would not be here was too awesome to consider for a moment. He was too far gone to realize that he'd come to the end of his nightmare . . . that any one of these loving friends would now look after his boy. But it was only the *Fraülein* he'd come to ask for help—only her face he longed to see.

She materialized in front of him like a vision in a dream. Hair askew, arms outstretched, tears coursing down her soot-smudged madonna's face.

He couldn't speak, but he knew she could read his heart. He handed her his precious son, and only then, as he watched his flesh and blood securely enveloped in her loving arms, did he give up the pretense of conscious thought.

Abruptly he passed out at her feet.

The next few days were surreal to Ruby. There were people to feed, children to entertain, plans to be made for every trying day. A posse was delegated to survey the valley; the dead were tallied and buried, the survivors reunited. Many of the burned-out settlers were parcelled out to the Caseys and three other ranches on the south side of the valley, but several families remained at the Barnetts'.

The men gathered to talk about money to be loaned and barns to be built and ranches to be abandoned altogether. Big families came first on the list; Orville told Ruby that the Morgens would have to wait their turn.

The women were busy with the logistics of feeding dozens of people with food and facilities that were barely enough for a single family. The long dry summer hadn't left them with any surplus, but no one begrudged the little they had.

Everyone made sacrifices; everyone reached out with love. Not one single settler was turned away. When Orville and Joshua ran out of cash for all those in need, C.W. Warren started arranging loans from his uncle's bank in Los Angeles. Word got around that Belinda Casey actually shared her own bedroom with three other ladies, and for several weeks the *Rancho* adobe was so full that Joshua gave up his own bed to sleep in the barn.

"If a straw bed was good enough for Jesus, it's good enough for me," he confessed to Ruby, who was deeply touched by the changes the fire had wrought in her friend.

And then there were the goodbyes. Some of the families—or parts of families in which the others had died—just didn't think it was worth the struggle. Who could predict the next fire or winter flood? Sarah Jasperson left the valley with the Hansons. The Carlsons, the Kentons, and the O'Rileys all said farewell. Orville and Clara decided that this scene of crisis was no place for their small children; once things settled down a bit, Ruby was to take Reed and Kathleen down to Phoebe's for a while. Susanna would stay to help out her mother. At two months short of thirteen, she would take her place as the youngest of the "women." Her childhood was another casualty of the fire.

Through it all, Kelby never left Ruby's side. He'd lost his joyful bouyancy, but she hoped that he was just tired from his recent illness and exhausting escape. Several times he'd told her about their terrifying flight from the fire. At break-neck speed they'd galloped the horses due south for an hour before Val had stepped in a hole and snapped a foreleg. She'd gone down on top of Wilhelm, who was so badly hurt he could barely pull the trigger of his Hawken. But he managed to put his beloved old horse to rest before the flames devoured her body. Kelby still wept when he talked about Val.

He saw little of his father while he stayed with Ruby, gaining more strength every day. Wilhelm spent the days working with the men and his nights seeking solace in some private communion with tired old Hedda. Although he sought out brief moments with Kelby, Wilhelm never tried to see Ruby alone. He thanked her for caring for his boy, but his gratitude was cautious and formal—and always when there were others present.

Finally Ruby could stand it no longer. She would soon be leaving for Los Angeles; she wanted to take Kelby with her, and she didn't want to leave his father until everything was straightened out between them.

"Wilhelm," she called to him one night when he came by the house to see Kelby, "do you think we could have some time to talk together? Tonight, perhaps, after the children are in bed?"

He lifted his eyes to hers sadly. "The Casey brothers rode back with us tonight. I imagine that Joshua will want to speak to you this evening."

"Whatever Joshua has to say to me can wait,

Wilhelm. I have something far more important to discuss with you. There is a question you asked me not so long ago that I . . . I don't believe I ever truly answered."

Carefully he pondered her shy, thoughtful words. His eyes studied every inch of her face as though he hadn't seen her in a very long time . . . or perhaps would never see her again. "*Fraülein,*" he finally replied, "I have something I must do tonight. Tomorrow will be soon enough for . . . questions and answers between us."

She took no comfort from the gravity of his tone, but at least he'd agreed on a time to talk. Yet Ruby went to bed wondering what lingering chore Wilhelm could possibly have that took precedence over asking her to become his wife.

"Aunt Clara said you wanted to see me, Uncle," Ruby announced as she stood in the doorway of the parlor early the next morning. She had dressed hurriedly, not because of anything her aunt had said, but because of the way she had said it. Urgency had colored the older woman's usually placid voice.

Orville stood up briefly as his niece entered the room, then settled back behind the big oak desk and motioned for Ruby to take a seat near him. "Don't look so frightened, honey. Nobody's going to rap your knuckles."

Ruby managed a thin laugh as she did as he asked. "I'm sorry. I'm just not used to being summoned at dawn for anything but starting breakfast. I don't believe I've ever seen you in the morning before you went to greet the chickens."

Her uncle smiled warmly, then leaned forward with his elbows on the desk. "I'm afraid they've already had that pleasure ahead of you today as well. But . . . I have something to tell you that it would be best to discuss before you greet our . . . numerous guests."

Something in his tone made Ruby stiffen. The group gathered in their fields and barns and upper rooms had no secrets from each other, and Orville Barnett was not a man who planned surreptitious intrigue.

"Is it . . . more bad news, Uncle?" she asked quietly, wondering how the news in Sycamore Valley could possibly get any worse.

"Well, I can't say I'm happy about everything that's happened since you went to bed last night, Ruby, but one piece of news is so glorious that I imagine it'll take care of any less cheerful tidings."

Ruby edged forward. For a man about to deliver glorious tidings, he didn't sound overwhelmed with joy. In fact, he sounded like a man who had to inform a dear friend that a loved one had just passed over to the other side.

"Joshua dropped by last night. He offered to drive you and the children down to Los Angeles in his best carriage. Seems to think it's a long ride in a stage."

Ruby took a quick breath. How thoughtful of Joshua! She had dreaded another stagecoach ride—dreaded leaving the valley altogether when Wilhelm and Kelby needed her so. "At times young Mr. Casey surprises me with his generosity," Ruby replied candidly.

Niece and uncle shared a knowing smile before Orville continued, "I'm afraid he does have an ulterior motive, Ruby. He told me quite frankly that he's afraid if you go to Los Angeles for any length of time, he might not be able to entice you back here. I guess the fire has made all of us give some thought to what matters to us the most, and in Joshua's case, that's you."

He paused to watched surprise wash over Ruby's face, then he added softly, "He seems to feel he's waited long enough to ask for your hand, honey. Last evening he requested permission to marry you . . . with all the humility and style any woman might wish. I was proud to give my consent."

Ruby didn't know what reaction her uncle expected of her, but she didn't have the strength to pretend she was pleased. Joshua was a good man, a kind man—not as kind as some, but kind enough nonetheless—and had she been free to love him, she might well have found a way to do just that. But visions of Wilhelm leading his lame horse swamped her eyes, and suddenly Ruby was choking back tears.

"Ah, a woman first and a Barnett second, I see," Orville commented dryly. "Do at least tell me I did the right thing before you babble, honey. Joshua will surely be coming by today and—"

"Oh, Uncle Orville!" she wept, despair flowing out of her with life-crushing force. "Don't you know how I feel? Don't you know that I like Joshua very, very much but for months now I've had Wilhelm's name engraved on my very soul?"

Orville closed his eyes and shook his head; then he crossed the space between them and touched her hair with a gentle hand. "Ah, Ruby, honey, I was afraid that was so. But it can't change a thing. Joshua wants to marry you. And Wilhelm . . . well—"

"Wilhelm does, too! He loves me, Uncle Orville. He needs me so very much, not just for Kelby, but for himself! He's too proud to tell me, but I know —"

She broke off at the look on her uncle's face. It was the look she'd seen on her own father's face so many years ago on the day she'd told him that her mother was only sleeping. Of course she'd wake up in the morning. . . .

For a minute neither of them spoke. They shared the silence and awesome tension of anticipated grief. But Orville already knew the story that would shatter his niece's hopes. She could only imagine his news with dread.

"Uncle—"

"Wilhelm's gone, honey. He rode out this morning. He bought Reed's pinto pony and a scrub horse he won't mind selling to a stranger in Los Angeles. He left Hedda here for you." He couldn't hide the wonder in his voice that Wilhelm had left his horse to a woman who could barely ride. "He asked me to handle the sale of his ranch to the railroad to finance his trip back to Germany."

Germany! The word bludgeoned her heart, destroying whatever comfort she might have taken from the fact that Wilhelm had left her his beloved mare. But Wilhelm's alarming decision to return to his homeland only confirmed the incontrovertible proof that the fire had broken the very spirit of the man Ruby loved. Had Uncle Orville really said that Wilhelm was *selling his ranch to the railroad*?

"Ruby, honey," her uncle repeated gently, "he's left the valley for good."

Ruby's stomach congealed in swift agony. The hardness took over her body in waves of nausea and pain. Her eyes glazed over; she shook her head in fierce denial.

"No. He would not leave without telling me goodbye. He would not leave me without some word!"

Orville looked like he'd been sent for and couldn't come; there was so little he could do to ease her pain. "He came to say goodbye to me last night. He didn't ask to speak to you, Ruby, or I would have sent someone to wake you." Not even the tenderness of his voice could dwarf the overwhelming hopelessness of his words. "He did leave something for you besides the mare, Ruby, but . . . it's hardly a wedding ring."

New hope filled her heart. Wilhelm would not leave her with a message . . . without a promise to return. Somehow, some way— "Let me see it. Please."

"Ruby, it isn't—"

"Let me see it!"

He shrugged and moved away, tugging open one of his old desk drawers. He pulled out a smooth chunk of manzanita and thrust it toward her. To him, it was meaningless. To Ruby, it was a rainbow after the storm that set Noah's arc adrift.

It was a carving, the style and care certain proof that it was a prize from Wilhelm's own hand. And because she'd seen him arrive with nothing but Kelby on his back, Ruby knew that somehow, in the commotion and chaos of practical survival that had prevailed in the last few days, pragmatic Wilhelm Morgen had stolen his last hours in the valley to create and refine this gift of beauty, this sentimental substitute for a lifetime of love with Ruby as his wife.

It was eight inches long and six inches high and its keyboard held four score and eight miniature keys. A single hymnal lay open on the delicate music stand that had been carved with such consummate care; faith and hope radiated from a handful of notes finely etched on the two tiny pages. It was the only thing Ruby had ever asked of Wilhelm—and the one thing he had sworn he would never be able to give her: music to fill her heart, music to uplift her soul.

Wilhelm had hoped to make good time during the cool of the day, but Kelby was already begging for rest by the time they reached the Tree. He could have taken a different trail to the main road to Los Angeles, but he knew that he could never have left the valley without saying goodbye to that part of himself which would always lie by the river.

The barn, of course, was completely gone, and the house was a pile of clay. The blackened soil held no trace of the crops he'd tended with such laborious care; even the Tree was charred for a good fifteen feet off the ground. Wilhelm took comfort in the discovery that it, at least, was still standing. The horses took comfort from the leafless shade it cast over the sooty, tepid water.

As he studied the scattered black remnants of his lifetime dream, Wilhelm decided to stop and rest a while. He knew it was important to pace the horses with care on such a long journey—important to pace the little one as well. *There is no great hurry anyway,* he reminded himself. *Why should a man rush home to announce his greatest failure to all those who once had such faith in him?*

He closed his eyes against the sun . . . against the pain. He knew it was more than the seeds of his own private dream he was leaving in this awesome valley. In this world of quail and mustard weed—in this nest of peace and quiet—he had found the one thing he had never dared hope for. A woman to heal his wounds, to greet his daily frowns with joy. A woman so strong and loving that she might have stood by him, even now, if he had given her the choice.

If there was any comfort to be gained in his defeat, it was in the knowledge that he had, at least, done what was best for the *Fraülein*. She deserved better than he could give her. She always had. But once he'd deluded himself into believing that his dreams would be enough; at least he could promise her a future. He would gain strength from the land

and hope from the Tree. He would carve a life for Kelby from this strange country. He would, somehow, justify Oma's great sacrifice for his sake.

Lies, he whipped himself. *It was a futile hope, a child's dream. God had other plans for me. I should be glad he only took my land and my future this time. At least my loved ones survived the fire.*

"Papa! Papa, someone is coming!" Kelby hollered, stopping his pinto pony in the middle of the dusty track. As his father halted his own horse and turned toward the spiralling dust, the boy continued, "Why is he riding so fast? It is too hot to make a horse run!"

Wilhelm spared a moment's smile for his tiny son. He would have made such a fine farmer. Even at six he knew the heart of his animals, knew his father's great love of the land.

But this was no time for looking backward. The horse was gaining on them, galloping at roping speed. Even at this distance the sweating chestnut coat glistened in the sunlight.

Suddenly he realized that he knew the horse. It was his own dear Hedda.

He knew the rider as well. By her billowing skirts he knew she was a woman — his woman — riding astride without a moment's concern for propriety, as though the west had claimed her once and for all. Her black hair streamed behind her as though she had not even put it up for the day.

"You will walk Hedda when she gets here," he commanded softly, ground-tying the horses by the stream as he dismounted. He spoke in German, using words to fill the emptiness in his heart; words as weapons to protect the *Fraülein* from his own selfish need of her. He must be strong enough to turn her away.

"The mare must be cool before she drinks and the

Fraülein and I will have to talk undisturbed. *Ja?*"

Kelby nodded quickly, but he stood silently by his father as he waited for *Fraülein* Ruby to come.

What will I say to her? Wilhelm's heart pounded unwillingly in his chest. *I was so sure she would understand.*

The *Fraülein's* halo-round face was flushed and sweating when she reached him. Determination shone from every pore as she slid to the ground and faced him squarely, her anguished eyes a mirror of his own.

For a moment she stood there defiantly, anger and fear doing battle for her heart. Then abruptly the anger dissolved and only the panic remained.

"Don't leave without me, Wilhelm!" she begged him, the words strangled by her deep, ragged breaths. "I'll live with you in a tent or a tree or on the open river, but I won't last a day if you leave me behind!"

He warred with his need to hold her; slowly he shook his head. Yet against his own will his fingertips reached out to cup her lovely face. He felt her tremble, saw the tears fill her beautiful brown eyes.

He tried to stand firm in his conviction, certain that he was right to decide her future. But when her tears spilled over and moistened his hand, his resistance collapsed in an instant.

"Ah, *Fraülein*!" he whispered. Helpless against the onrush of feelings, he wrapped both his arms around her and pulled her close against his chest. "Don't you understand? I love you too much to take you with me. I have nothing to give you now, not even promises. My dreams lie buried in the ashes."

She clung to him tightly, her tears glistening in his scraggly beard. "Then pick them up and dust them off, Wilhelm!" she sobbed against his neck. "You have a woman who would do anything for you; you have a precious child. You have a ranch that can be rebuilt no matter how many times nature takes it from you, and you have wonderful people showing you the bounty of God's love." Her loving brown eyes begged him to understand. "You see the fire, Wilhelm, and your house burned to the ground. But I see people holding out their hands to you who turned their backs before; I see a community which has learned that love is all that matters."

Bravely she moved her hands to touch his face, her tenderness moving him beyond all earthly words. Her urgency made him ache to please her.

"You wanted to build a church, Wilhelm! Well, we've got a church here now. We don't have a scrap of spare lumber or even an uncut log, but we have people who hold on to each other in prayer and praise. Jesus is with us as he never was before!" She pressed herself back against him, and he clung to her with an anguish that was new to him and completely overwhelming. Even Oma's death paled against the loss of this incredible woman.

"Don't give it up, Wilhelm!" she begged him, her lips nuzzling his torn and smoky shirt. "Don't throw it all away! If you leave Sycamore Valley now, you'll never be a whole man again."

He rested his chin on the top of her head, fighting a mist in his eyes that reflected the tears in her own. It was a struggle to frame words in English. "This I know already, *Fraülein*. But I cannot stay here and watch you start your marriage to Joshua Casey." His voice was low and ragged. "Surely this you know."

Ruby pulled back to face him squarely. "Surely *you* know that I would never marry Joshua when my heart belongs to you!"

His blue eyes grew dark and intense; his fingertips laced her long black hair, knotted by her wild ride.

"Yes, this I know so very well, *Fraülein.* But you will forget me sooner if I go."

"Forget you? Wilhelm, it would take forever—"

"It would take even longer to build another house by the Tree, *Fraülein*, even if I could bring myself to ask Joshua or your uncle to help me get a loan. I cannot ask you to wait that long."

"Then don't make me wait!" Ruby pleaded. "I want to stand beside you, Wilhelm. I want to be your helpmate, not a burden!"

The smile he gave her—tender and tired—made it clear that to him she was anything but a burden. For a moment he stood there, searching for his reasons for leaving the valley—so reasonable just a few minutes ago—but nothing came to mind. All he could see was the fire in her eyes, the determination in her mouth, the love and desperation that kept her trembling in his arms. He could not see the house in ashes anymore.

"Papa, Hedda is cool now and I am very tired. Can I sit down under the Tree?"

Slowly he lowered his gaze to his small son. The boy stood in the barest hint of a trail amidst acres and acres of parched, blackened soil. His only shelter was the massive sycamore Tree; his only friends the three tired horses which encircled his father . . . and the woman who now loved him like a son. Was this to be his future? Was this really a better place to start a life than on an eastbound ship or the crowded streets of Los Angeles?

"Go rest under the Tree," Wilhelm told the boy with sudden determination. He was done blaming God for his problems; done blaming himself for Oma's tragic death. He was ready to celebrate the blessings that the Lord had showered upon him, starting with this incredible woman who had surely been sent to heal his wounds. "We will go back to see your small friend Reed in just a little while."

Kelby let out a whoop that startled the horses, then restrained his joy as he read the solemnity of his father's face. "Yes, Papa. Of course, Papa! I will take care of the horses, Papa!"

In a flash the boy and horses disappeared. Wilhelm turned his eyes from the Tree to the woman, his expression grave and humble. "You will go on to Los Angeles with your uncle's children as he has planned. I will do what I have to do to build a life here for my family."

Ruby stared at him uncertainly. "When you say 'your family,' do you mean—"

"I mean my wife and my child."

Ruby closed her eyes and bit her lips in anguished relief. Once again he pulled her closer. For a moment neither one could speak, but words were not necessary for what their hearts had to say.

"I should say my wife and my children, *Fraülein*," Wilhelm managed to whisper into her hair. "I hope the Lord will bless us with many others."

"Oh, Wilhelm!" Ruby breathed against him. "I'll get the children settled with Phoebe and come back just as soon as I can. I can take a list of things we'll need and—"

"No."

Again she froze, her tenacious hold on his neck tense and uncertain. For a moment she was silent once more. Then she murmured, "I think . . . I think maybe I did not fully understand you, Wilhelm."

He pulled back to face her, his eyes warm but as determined as her own. "I am asking only that you wait for me, *Fraülein*. I cannot ask you to be my wife while I have not so much as a roof to put over your head! But I promise that I will send for you as soon as I have built a house that is fit for a bride. A house full of 'flowers and music and light.' "

She hung her head at the bitter memory of her own hasty words. "Oh, Wilhelm, surely you know I don't need anything fancy! I just want to be with you. I don't want you to be alone anymore!"

A smile glorified his rugged features. "I do not think I will be alone this time, *Fraülein*. There are now 'two or three gathered' in His name in Sycamore Valley, and I will take my place 'in the midst of them.' " His smile enveloped her completely. "If Someone were not looking after me, *Fraülein*, I do not think you would have come to bring me back."

At last he'd found an answer that Ruby could not refute. She put her arms around him while he held her as tightly as he dared. "I think you're quite right, Wilhelm. I can go to Los Angeles for a little while. You will no longer be alone here."

They held each other closer yet, rocking together in the light coastal zephyr that suddenly bathed the valley with fresh hope.

At length Ruby met Wilhelm's determined blue eyes and whispered prayerfully, "May the Lord watch between me and thee, while we are absent, one from the other."

And Wilhelm answered in German, "*Amen.*"

Anger and fear fled to the mountains. Under the Tree there was only love.

EPILOGUE

The train moved smoothly forward. The heavy chug-a-chug-a, chug-a-chug-a sound beneath her was like the comfort of a well-loved country song . . . not because it was intrinsically beautiful, but because it reminded her of how close she finally was to the people she loved.

What a long year it had been! Not once since Wilhelm had returned Ruby to her uncle's ranch had she seen his beloved, craggy face; not once had she held little Kelby in her arms. Los Angeles was close enough that they could have seen each other once or twice, but Wilhelm had insisted that he could not bear to see her for just a day or two when he could not bring her home. She understood his thinking, but still his willingness to wait so long—to fix everything on Morgen land to his satisfaction before they married—was difficult to bear. His last few delays had not made sense to Ruby, and she had wondered, more than once, if he were truly as eager as she was for their wedding to take place.

Wilhelm's letters were few and far between—sparse and practical like the man himself—but the glowing embers beneath his brief words had sustained her during the early months of their separation.

"It is not so hard as I imagined," he'd written once, telling her that he'd gone ahead with his dreams of planting orange trees instead of reseeding the fields with barley. "The others help me, and this time I am building not a house but a home." Later, he'd added, "Today I dug ditches with Jesus by my side. To think of all the years I picked up the shovel alone!"

But the letter she cherished most had arrived just before Christmas, almost six months ago. "You cannot know how much I miss you, *Fraülein*," her stoic love had admitted. "Please do not stop waiting for me."

"Sycamore! Sycamore next station stop!" the conductor hollered, his bright red uniform as cheerful as his voice.

Ruby took a moment to retie her slate cap, then brushed off her crisp blue gown as she reveled in the ease of modern train travel. How peaceful was this confusion compared to her memories of the jostling stage over this same rough stretch of country! Off to the south—far, far to the south—she caught a glimpse of the tall, scraggly branches of the massive Tree that had welcomed her to the valley such a long time ago. But today the train would not deliver her to Wilhelm's front door. One corner of Sarah Jasperson's ranch had been platted as the new town of Sycamore—a small but growing community with its very own railroad depot. Wilhelm had written that Sycamore also had a general store, a telegraph office, and a sporadic newspaper, put out by none other than Joshua Casey, who now held weekly prayer meetings in his office.

But Ruby's excitement as the buildings came into view was miniscule compared to her longing to see the man who would soon claim her as his wife. His last letter had been his briefest, and the one that had renewed her dwindling hope. "*Fraülein*, if you have time to come to Sycamore to visit your uncle, I would like to come calling. I have a question I am now at liberty to ask."

She had wired him an answer in less than an hour and left Los Angeles the very next day. A lifetime ago in Cincinnati, she would have considered it unseemly to rush so breathlessly to such a summons. But after so many months apart she would have galloped to Wilhelm on horseback or run to him on foot! She would even have braved a stage.

Ruby didn't recognize him at once. It was partly the crush of people on the sidewalks . . . and the hazy background of crude public buildings made of brick and knotty pine. There were more people in this one block of Sycamore than had lived in the whole valley a year ago! Joshua had always said that the railroad would change the valley forever, but she had not understood. She had never fully understood Joshua, who wore most of his heart on the outside, just as Wilhelm kept his soul tucked safely inside his vest.

Today he was not only wearing a vest, but a fresh new suit with a felt hat and a tie! Yes . . . yes it really was Wilhelm! With a trim, short beard? And a haircut? Even his black boots were polished!

For a moment his appearance frightened Ruby. She'd been gone a long time. Could Wilhelm have changed somehow—changed into someone who was no longer right for her? Coupled with his recent delays, it was a frightening thought.

And then she saw his face, his kind blue eyes, his

desperately tense expression and hunched shoulders . . . his toes straining against the shining new storebought leather. Suddenly her heart was in tune with his again. Hadn't she bought a special dress just for this trip . . . and another one for the wedding? Hadn't she made little Kelby a new shirt, which he was wearing with such pride right now? It was neatly buttoned and tucked into trim little pants that hung clear down to his ankles; his brown hair was slicked back and he wore a smile that consumed most of his face.

"Papa!" he yelled without compunction when he saw Ruby. "It's the *Fraülein*! There she is!"

Wilhelm nodded gravely, nervously, before he met her eyes. He stepped forward to help Ruby off the train, but he made no other move to welcome her.

Kelby did. Wriggling like a puppy, he thrust a tiny nosegay of poppies and monkey flowers against her dress as he threw his arms around her. "Oh, *Fraülein* Ruby! I'm so glad you're back! Promise me you'll never go away again!"

Ruby knelt to hug the child, tears filling her eyes as she remembered the day of her first uncertain arrival in the valley when she'd met this man and child. How wonderful to be greeted so! She had missed Kelby greatly, and it was no effort to share his ebullient embrace. But somewhere deep within her she heard herself crying. *It should be Wilhelm who is greeting me like this. Has he changed his mind? Have I become another obligation to him . . . a promise he made in the midst of his pain?*

Slowly she straightened and met Wilhelm's eyes. They were dark, guarded, unreadable. "You are . . . well, *Fraülein*?" he asked stiffly.

Wordlessly she nodded.

"And the train . . . it was easier for you than the stage coach?"

"Yes. Much easier, Wilhelm." His words gave her a breath of comfort. So he still remembered their strange first meeting. He'd never been one to brandish his feelings publically. Maybe he was just waiting until they could be alone. . . .

"Your uncle asked for me to meet you. A habit, perhaps, from the days when there was no stop for the stage." From another man it would have been a joke, but Wilhelm looked so serious that Ruby didn't know what to make of his remark. When she didn't answer, Wilhelm shifted his glance uncomfortably and added, "He would have come for you himself, *Fraülein*, but he thought . . . I thought . . . that you would be expecting me."

This time their eyes met, and Ruby struggled to tell him the truth. "I have been waiting for over a year, Wilhelm. When I got your last letter I assumed that . . . that the waiting was over and nothing had changed between us." She swallowed hard. "Was I wrong?"

Relief washed over his rough-hewn face like a rainbow after a storm. "I have counted the days, *Fraülein*," he confessed, his voice low and strained. "It is just that . . . to look at you . . . so beautiful, so fresh from the city . . . I am afraid that even after all I have done, it will not be enough. You deserve so much more than I can ever give you."

Ruby shook her head, annoyed and relieved. "What I deserve is your faith in me, Wilhelm. I would have lived with you in the ashes! Whatever home you've built will be more than enough for me. All I want is your love and your name. And your promise that we won't ever have to be apart like this again."

For several moments he studied her face. Then he whispered gravely, "That promise you now have." He reached down to tousle his son's perfectly combed hair and added, "Kelby could not bear it." And this time he gave her the ghost of a smile.

Cautiously she smiled back, and Wilhelm took her arm as he led her toward the wagon. She recognized dear old Hedda, but the other horse was new. "Papa says you can ride Hedda whenever you want to," Kelby told her when his father went back for her trunk. "Unless she needs to be plowing the fields."

"I'd like that, Kelby. Are you still riding your pony?"

"Oh yes, *Fraülein*! And now I have a dog. There is so much to show you! The house is—"

"The house is to be a surprise, *Kleines-Bärchen*," Wilhelm admonished the boy gently as he climbed up beside Ruby. "The *Fraülein* will see it soon enough."

Ruby met his eyes briefly. "Are you . . . going to show me the house on our way to Uncle Orville's?"

He took the reins and studied her for a moment, his eyes dark and subdued. And then, quite suddenly, the sun rose on his face and bathed her with dawn's fresh warmth and light. "Ah, yes, *Fraülein*. I would like very much to show you our new home."

Ruby grinned, her whole body suddenly buoyant and joyful. This was the Wilhelm she loved; careful with his feelings, but oh, how deep they ran! "There's nothing I'd like better, Wilhelm."

He hardly took his eyes off her from the town to the ranch; the horses could have made the trip without him. Kelby chattered over every mile, pointing out new citrus seedlings and other crops they had planted. He seemed oblivious to the undercurrents of new bonding between the grownups on either side of him. Ruby still longed for a moment alone with Wilhelm, but she was no longer afraid. She was home—utterly and completely at home for the first time since her father had died—and she no longer had the slightest doubt about the warmth of her welcome.

"There it is!" Kelby shouted as a distant house came into view. "What do you think of it, *Fraülein?*"

At first Ruby could not answer. Even a mile away, it was evident that Wilhelm had not rebuilt the simple pioneer's hut that the fire had swept away. A white-washed second story loomed above a trim veranda just like Uncle Orville's. There was real glass in the windows! Orange and yellow calico curtains, surely made by Aunt Clara's loving hand, fluttered in the breeze. And all around the porch—in bold declaration of a promise made and kept—stood bright golden sunflowers almost six feet tall! It was not a single man's shanty, a homesteader's excuse for survival. It was a home for a family . . . for Ruby and Wilhelm's children, and someday Kelby's children, and his children's children after that!

"Oh, Wilhelm!" she breathed, unable to find any other words to voice her joy. "Oh, Wilhelm!"

He and Kelby shared a grin. "I helped Papa plant the flowers!" the little boy informed her proudly. "They need water every day when it is this hot. Papa says it will be my special job all the time!"

Ruby put her arm around Kelby and gave him a tender hug, "You did a wonderful job, sweetheart. And so did your papa."

Wilhelm flashed her a glowing smile as he pulled up to the door. "You take her in and show her around, Kelby. I'm going to water the horses before we go on to Orville's."

Wilhelm helped Ruby off the wagon, his hands trembling as he held her near for just a second. How keenly she shared his longing for a kiss! But that special moment must come when they were alone, and Kelby was not about to take a step from her side.

"I will be back in a moment, *Fraülein*," Wilhelm promised.

Kelby grabbed Ruby's hand and tugged her into the kitchen. It had a fine wood stove and a huge family dining table. He dragged her up the stairs to see where "my brothers who aren't here yet will sleep with me." There was another room for the girls, and a room for Ruby and Wilhelm that already had a beautiful green patchwork Tree of Life quilt laid out on the double bed—another gift from Clara and the girls.

Before Ruby could begin to absorb the wonders of Wilhelm's painstaking creation, Kelby towed her down the stairs again. "You must see the parlor, *Fraülein*! It is a special surprise. If it were not for the train we could not have done it at all. It took eight teams of horses to get it from there to here and—"

The boy cut off as Ruby gasped in disbelief. The parlor itself was unremarkable—nicely furnished for a western home, with some of Wilhelm's carvings near the fire. But in one corner—the farthest corner from the fire—stood a real-life version of the last gift Wilhelm had created for her . . . the tiny carving that had been a promise in more ways than one. Somehow he had brought her a full-size upright piano!

Ruby blinked furiously and bit her lip as waves of tenderness tossed her heart. A waste of good kindling, he'd called it. A waste of time and money. He'd borrowed cash and six teams of horses and trundled this beautiful instrument over miles of rocks and chaparral! And she had doubted the depth of his feelings!

Ruby shook her head and edged closer to the incredible gift of love. A picture of her father—one she'd left with Orville—stood enshrined in a hand-carved frame atop the instrument. On the other end perched a stack of hymnals—familiar ones that Ruby had hauled by stage all the way from Cincinnati. And on the music stand, lying open and ready to be played, was her favorite songbook turned to hymn number 141: "All Hail the Power of Jesus' Name."

Tears were streaming down Ruby's face when she heard Wilhelm step into the room behind her. Slowly she turned to face the man who had crowned her life with such unexpected joy, helpless to express her love and gratitude with human speech.

Wilhelm's face was so full of devotion that no words were necessary between them, yet it was obvious that he still wanted to say whatever it might be that Ruby needed to hear. But he could not sputter out a single tender word before she flew across the room into his arms.

"*Fraülein*," he whispered against her hair as she crushed against him. "I am not a man of words, but . . . you know, yes, *Fraülein*?"

Ruby clung to him, kissing his cheek in an anguished moment of relief and promise before she remembered that they were not alone. She glanced down to see little Kelby standing beside them, his shining face uplifted as he wrapped one small stubby hand around each pair of grownup knees. As Ruby lowered her hand to include the child in their embrace, her fingertips met Wilhelm's as he reached to do the same.

Kelby grinned from ear to ear, thrilled to be included in their circle of love. Above their child, Wilhelm's eyes met Ruby's, but neither tried to talk. They both knew that there were no questions left to ask, and none left to be answered.